CAPE MAY MAGIC

CLAUDIA VANCE

CHAPTER ONE

Margaret walked through a large garden plot full of colorful flowers with the hot summer breeze blowing her long brown hair up off her shoulders. She took a deep breath, inhaling the floral aromas wafting through the air as she pulled a pair of pruners from her suede gardening fanny pack, before dead-heading some sunflowers that had fallen victim to having all their seeds plucked out by birds.

"It looks great out here, doesn't it?" Dave asked, feeling impressed as he waded through the tall rows of flowers in the cutting garden that Margaret had planted two months earlier.

All around them stood yellow and orange sunflowers of various heights, poppies in bright purples, reds, and oranges, dinner plate dahlias, tall snapdragons, a rainbow of zinnias, ranunculus, and much more. Off to the side was her butterfly garden full of pink flowering common milkweed, bright-purple coneflowers, and bee balm. It was a gardener's paradise.

Margaret smiled at Dave, then stopped to gaze at a trellis of flowering sweet peas. The green leaves and stems covered the structure, making the fragrant pastel pink and purple blooms pop. "It's better than I could have imagined. I've never had much luck with a lot of these flowers in the past, like these sweet peas. They would get eaten by rabbits when they were tiny seedlings before they could mature and flower."

Dave wiped the sweat off his forehead with the back of his arm. "You never had much luck with the larkspur either, and look at them go," he said, pointing at the tall blue, white, purple, and pink flowering stalks held up by twine between six-foot wooden stakes.

"You're right, and I can't believe how easy they were to grow. I simply sprinkled the larkspur seeds on the dirt in early spring, and as soon as the weather warmed, they took off. One of the easiest things I've grown," Margaret said.

Dave smiled. "I'll say. You sure made this garden gorgeous this year. Can you believe this is our second summer here? This year, we actually have time to do these gardens right."

Margaret sighed happily as she took off her gardening gloves and wrapped her arm around Dave's shoulders. Dave put his arm around her waist, and they both looked over the flower field together, feeling proud of and impressed with their work.

"I had Dale and Donna's wedding in mind when I planted these. I think it will be a perfect backdrop for some bridal photos," Margaret said.

"Oh, definitely. What about the floral arrangements for the tables?" Dave asked.

Margaret cocked her head to the side. "Well, thankfully, Donna hired a florist for that. I don't think I'm that great at putting together bouquets, but maybe I'll try my hand at a few to put in some random places if there's time."

Dave laughed. "We're going to have our hands pretty full getting the property ready, helping people park, and making sure the vendors know where to set up."

Margaret shook her head and laughed. "My gosh, we're going to be busy. I feel like there was way less going on for our wedding."

"Maybe that's because our wedding was a surprise to all of the guests," Dave said nudging Margaret playfully.

Margaret shrugged. "Maybe, but boy, putting together a surprise wedding is also a lot of work."

Dave looked up at the sky and noticed how hazy it now appeared, muting the sun behind it.

"What is that? Smoke?" Margaret asked looking up alongside Dave.

"It's gotta be those forest fires up in North Jersey," Dave said, shaking his head in disbelief, as he reached into his pocket, noticing an unknown call was coming through on his phone.

Margaret headed over to the vegetable garden as Dave took the call.

"Hello?" Dave said as he answered his phone.

"Hi. Is this Dave Patterson?" a woman's voice asked.

"Yes, it is," Dave said as he headed in Margaret's direction.

"Hi, I'm Joyce from Fox Run Wildlife Refuge in East Orange. I got your phone number after calling Pinetree Wildlife Refuge. I hope you don't mind me calling, but I think we desperately need your help," she said with some urgency behind her voice.

Dave stopped dead in his tracks. "You're kidding. What's going on?"

"Well, the forest fires are going on. It looks to be somewhat contained now, but we've had hundreds of acres of land affected and tons of hurt and displaced animals that need enclosures while they recuperate. We've never had a situation like this, so we've been calling around South Jersey to find help. Your name came up a lot. You must be pretty good," Joyce said as she walked around the refuge's property, eyeing up all the animals. "We fashioned up some temporary makeshift enclosures, but they can't stay in them long. They're not big enough, and they're not secure enough to keep them in and predators out. Would you be willing to come help? We've got a room in a

3

house on the land you can stay in, and there's a team of volunteers that will be helping you build things. We just need someone who knows what they're doing to lead the way."

Dave rubbed his hands on his face, not sure of what to say. "Wow. OK, I'd like to help, but let me first get the approval from my boss—"

Joyce cut him off. "Oh, your boss is who gave me your number. She said they'd be willing to part with you for about a week or so if that works for you. We kind of need you immediately. I have a feeling a lot more wildlife will be brought in before the end of the night."

Dave looked over at Margaret, who was now smiling at him from behind the cucumber trellis. "OK, let me give you a call back in about ten minutes, Joyce. I have one more person I need to run this by."

Joyce nodded. "That's totally fine. I get it. Talk soon," she said as they both hung up.

Dave came up behind Margaret and pulled a small pickling cucumber off the vine, brushed it off, and took a bite and swallowed, savoring the cooling crispness of it.

"Who was on the phone?" Margaret asked as she pulled off another cucumber and took a bite.

"A wildlife refuge up north, Fox Run. Pinetree gave them my number. They're desperate for help with building animal enclosures for all the animals that were hurt, lost their homes, or became orphaned in the fire. They need me for the next week or so," Dave said, starting to feel a little stressed about the situation.

Margaret finished eating her cucumber and turned to look Dave square in the eyes. "You should do it. They need your help."

Dave looked around the property. "What about all the prep work for the wedding? I have to mow all of these acres. We have to get our land ready for the nuptials. You shouldn't do that all on your own. You can't possibly do that on your own."

Margaret sighed and shrugged. "Well, I'll be fine, and you'll be back before the wedding, right?"

Dave nodded. "Definitely. I'll make sure of that, but I really don't like leaving you alone to handle all this right now. I think it's too much."

Margaret wrapped her arm around Dave's waist, and out of the corner of her eye, way across the way, she spied their neighbor outside in his yard. "Look, there he is," she said, trying to point discreetly.

Dave gazed across their property, squinting to get a better look. "How have we not met our neighbor yet?"

Margaret watched as the eighty-five-year-old frail-looking man in a plaid shirt and hat walked hunched over towards his bird feeder across the yard full of birds, squirrels, and chipmunks that immediately scattered away. He then took off the top of the feeder and lifted a heavy bag of birdseed, pouring it ever so carefully to fill it back up. As he headed back inside, he stopped to look towards Margaret and Dave. Before Margaret could wave at him, he was back inside, the screen door slamming behind him.

"Well, he seems interesting. He sure likes those critters," Dave said with a chuckle.

Margaret laughed. "I like him. Any man who has a heart for animals is good in my book," she said as she gazed lovingly at Dave.

Dave blushed and wrapped his arm around Margaret. "I'm going to call work to figure out when I'm returning to Pinetree before calling Joyce back. I have a feeling I'm leaving tonight or tomorrow. It sounds like they're about to be even more overloaded. You sure you'll be OK with me not being here the next week or so?"

Margaret waved her hand in the air. "I'll be fine. I think it's important that you go help those animals in need. I know Fox Run Wildlife Refuge needs all the support right now," she said turning to look back at their neighbor's house. "Do you think he saw us looking over at him? I mean all this land makes us quite a bit away from his house."

Dave shrugged. "Maybe? Why?"

"I don't know. For some reason, I feel bad for him. Maybe he's lonely over there? Every time we've stopped over to introduce ourselves, he's never been home. I hope he doesn't think we're avoiding him," Margaret said.

Dave nodded. "Well, we've been here a year and still have yet to meet him. How about when I get home from Fox Run, we'll find a way to finally introduce ourselves. We can see if we can help him out with anything."

Margaret gave a sigh of relief. "That sounds great," she said as she glanced at the tomato plants next to them. There were rows and rows of tomatoes planted with stakes and Florida weaved with twine. The bright-green tomatoes glistened in the hazy sunlight.

Dave noticed Margaret looking at the tomatoes and ran his hand along a branch, then smelled his fingers. "That tomato smell is so intoxicating. I don't think anything smells more like a Jersey summer."

Margaret nodded. "That and the smell of the beach. It doesn't get much better."

* * *

Over at Westside Market, Judy stood in line to order sandwiches.

"Are you waiting for something?" a gentleman behind the counter asked.

"I haven't ordered yet, but I'm going to take one Godfather and one Jersey Girl, please," Judy said as she eyed up the deli meats in the case.

The man pointed towards the kiosk. "I'll get that going for you, but make sure to put in your sandwich orders over there first."

6

Judy backed away from the counter to head towards the kiosk when she almost stepped on someone behind her. "Oh my, I'm so sorry. I didn't see you there. I probably shouldn't walk backwards," Judy said while laughing.

The other woman laughed. "I do it all the time. No worries," she said while studying Judy's face. "Wait a minute. Do I know you? Judy?"

Judy cocked her head to the side. "Noreen? Is that you?" Judy asked, surprised.

The women, feeling pleasantly shocked to run into each other, hugged.

"I haven't seen you in forever!" Judy exclaimed.

Noreen nodded. "You and I were the best front desk staff at Dr. Malone's, that's for sure. I left not too long after you did."

Judy smiled and shook her head. "Gosh, I can't believe that was, what? Thirty years ago?"

Noreen hugged Judy again. "Why did we ever lose touch?"

Judy shrugged. "I don't know, but I'm sure it had to do with us both having active kids that made our lives very busy," she said as she typed in her order at the kiosk.

"Well, give me your number. Maybe we can get lunch sometime," Noreen said as she took her phone out of her purse.

They swapped phone numbers, and before they knew it, their sandwiches were ready.

Judy grabbed hers after Noreen. "Bob is obsessed with the Godfather. Says it's the best thing since sliced bread," Judy said with a chuckle.

Noreen laughed. "That's funny. I also picked up my husband's favorite. The Skinny Dip."

They both paid and headed out to the parking lot together.

Noreen's car was parked next to Judy's. She stopped as she was about to open the door. "I forgot to ask what you're up to these days."

Judy smiled. "Living the retired life. We usually always find things to do. You?"

Noreen nodded. "Same. I watch my grandkids here and there, but I've become a Cape May beach tag checker. I love it. We're actually looking for someone to fill in a few weekdays over the next couple of weeks. Are you interested?"

Judy's eyes lit up. "That actually sounds … fun. I think I may be interested."

"Do you like sitting on the beach and talking to people?" Noreen asked.

"Of course," Judy said, laughing.

"Well, you'll be doing that plus collecting money and giving out beach tags. Bring an umbrella and a chair, and you're set," Noreen said.

"Well, then, sign me up," Judy exclaimed.

"Perfect. I'll give you a call, and we'll go over everything later today," Noreen said as she opened the car door and plopped into the driver's seat. "It was so good running into you."

"Agreed. Enjoy those sandwiches," Judy said as she got into her car. Before putting the key in the ignition, she called Bob, who picked the phone up right away. "Hey, dear. I'll be home shortly with lunch," she said after Bob answered.

"Perfect, I just returned from picking up some drinks at Ostara's Coffee House, and you'll never believe what I did," Bob said excitedly.

The car was getting hot, so Judy finally turned the key and cranked the air-conditioning. "What was that?"

Bob sighed as he took a sip of his cold brew coffee. "For some reason there weren't any parking spots left near Ostara's, so I had to park near the Animal Outreach of Cape May County. Can you believe after all these years, I've never been there?"

Judy squinted in thought. "I don't think I have either. It's a shelter, right?"

Bob nodded. "Yes, and a wonderful one at that. They're no-kill and really rely on the help of volunteers. I signed up to go in a couple days a week on a whim."

"That's wonderful, Bob. I'm sure they'll appreciate any help they can get," Judy said, beaming with pride. "What kind of stuff will you be doing?"

Bob scratched his chin. "I'm not exactly sure, but I heard laundry, cleaning, feeding, petting, and driving the cats to vet appointments."

Judy smiled. "Well, I ran into my old coworker Noreen at Westside Market just now. She's a beach tag checker and asked me if I'd like to fill in a few days a week over the next couple of weeks. I said yes."

Bob laughed. "We really can't sit still, can we? Always have to be off doing something."

CHAPTER TWO

"Come on out here so I can see," Donna's mom, Janet, said.

Donna stepped out of the dressing room in a tiered bridal gown. "Mom, I absolutely hate it," Donna said as she twirled in front of the floor-length mirrors before her.

Janet made a face of annoyance. "What's wrong with it? I think it looks great."

Donna stared into the mirror, not recognizing the person she was looking at. "It's just not *me*. I don't feel like myself in this dress. I look like someone else."

Janet sighed and shook her head. "Well, it's coming down to the wire, Donna. You've got less than two weeks until the wedding. You're going to be wearing a sundress from the mall if you don't find something soon."

Donna sighed and plopped into a nearby chair, the long dress overtaking the floor before her. "I don't know what I'm going to do. This is the seventh bridal store we've been to. The fun has come and gone at this point. Heck, I've already done the mimosas, brunch, and dress shopping with the girls, and nothing came of that either. I feel like I'm not going to find anything at this point."

"If you need any kind of alterations, it's too late to hire

someone. It will probably be me doing it last minute, and that might get a little hectic," Janet said as she stood up to look at some other dresses on a nearby rack, starting to feel stressed herself.

Donna's phone chimed with a notification. She stood from the chair, gathered the train of her dress, and ran to her purse in the dressing room.

"Are you expecting a call?" Janet asked, wondering what the emergency was.

Donna shook her head as she used her finger to scroll on the screen. "No, but I have weather notifications set up. We're almost to the ten-day forecast, but so far, it's looking like nice, sunny weather leading up to the wedding. I hope it stays that way."

Janet nodded. "I hope so too, especially since the wedding is outdoors."

"How's everything going over here?" the owner of the bridal shop asked as she looked Donna up and down. "That dress is a favorite among our brides. It looks stunning on you."

Donna gulped. "It is … quite stunning. I just don't think it's what I'm looking for. I can't put my finger on it, but I guess I have to keep looking," she said as she headed back to the dressing room.

Janet smiled at the owner to break the awkwardness. "Lovely shop you've got here. We've never been. This is my daughter's *second* marriage, but she found her dress in California the first time," Janet whispered.

"Oh, is that so?" the owner asked.

Donna, overhearing, rolled her eyes from the dressing room as she took the dress off.

Janet nodded and held her hands over her mouth to mute what she was saying. "We're hoping this man is the *one* this time."

* * *

Over at Donna's Restaurant, Dale was filling in behind the bar for an afternoon shift after the bartender called out sick. He took a rag from his back pocket and wiped down the top of the bar when a customer wearing a tan suit jacket with slicked-back hair walked in and took a seat at the end of the bar.

Before Dale could even greet the man, a customer sitting at a table in the dining room got up and approached the gentleman. Dale couldn't hear what was being said but saw them shake hands and start talking. Next thing he knew, another customer got up to shake hands and talk with him.

Dixie, one of the restaurant's managers, walked up and stood next to Dale, looking over at the man sitting at the bar. "Why does that guy look familiar?"

Dale shook his head. "He doesn't look familiar to me, but apparently he does to a lot of people in here. They keep coming up to him to shake hands and talk. Did we get a new mayor or something?" he asked jokingly.

Carlos walked out of the kitchen, swinging his white apron over his shoulder. "Guys, I'm out. Derek is in there taking over the kitchen now. Wait a minute…" he said staring at the man at the bar. "Is that … Jack Jeffries?"

"That's him!" Dixie yelled loudly, startling almost everyone in the restaurant, before ducking behind the bar. "Oh, jeez. He heard me, didn't he?"

Dale laughed as Dixie stood back up and composed herself.

Carlos rested his forearm on Dale's shoulder as they stared towards Jack. "Jack Jeffries. He's one of the best magicians of all time."

"Never heard of him," Dale said as he started cleaning some dirty glasses in the bar sink.

Dixie widened her eyes in disbelief. "You've never heard of him? My gosh, he was on that show … what was it called?"

"*Behind the Curtain: Deciphering a Magician's Secrets*," Carlos said proudly. "I've seen every episode."

Dale shrugged. "Guess I don't watch enough TV. Never heard of him or the show."

Just then, Jack was finally alone, so Dale grabbed a menu, then headed over to greet him with Dixie and Carlos following behind.

"How ya doing today?" Dale said as he placed the menu in front of Jack, who seemed to be dressed for winter in the heat of the summer.

"Doing great," Jack said as he studied the menu. "I'd order a Manhattan, but it's too early, and I've got a show tonight. Better stick to an iced tea for now," he said with a smile. "Also, give me one of your cheeseburgers I've been hearing about. Cooked medium is good," he said as he handed the menu back to Dale.

Dixie playfully pushed Dale aside as she propped her elbows on the bar. Carlos followed suit. "Mr. Jack Jeffries. I never thought I'd see the day that you'd be here in Cape May. What brings you to our shore town?"

Jack cocked his head to the side. "Oh, you didn't hear? I'm over at the Cape May Movie Theater tonight. Doing a pretty big show on the stage over there."

Carlos playfully nudged Dixie aside. "You're kidding. Hey, you mind signing something for my daughter real quick? She loves you," Carlos asked as he looked around for a pen and something to sign. He quickly grabbed a napkin from the stack on the bar.

Dale filled a glass with iced tea, put a lemon wedge on the rim, and headed back to Jack with it, noticing he was signing his name on a napkin and handing it to Carlos.

"You're the best. Hope to catch your show sometime," Carlos said as he walked past Dale and gave him the widest grin anyone had ever seen.

"Well, I'll let you enjoy your drink," Dixie said, as she started walking away. "It was nice meeting you."

Now it was just Dale and Jack there. Dale scratched his

chin. "Your burger should be out shortly. Anything else I can get ya for the time being?"

Jack shook his head. "I think I'm good, thank you."

Dale started to walk away but stopped. "I have to say, I didn't know who you were, but everyone else seems to know. I think I'm too far removed from television and social media. You're a magician, eh?"

Jack tapped his fingers on the bar. "Yep. Kind of followed in my dad's footsteps. Never thought I'd be where I am now with it. It's quite mind-boggling."

"That's really cool. I'm happy for you. I don't think I've ever seen a magic show," Dale said, noticing more customers taking seats at the bar.

"Never?" Jack asked, astonished.

Dale shook his head. "Nope. I guess I always thought magic shows were only for kids. I never thought anything of it."

Jack shifted his eyes. "Let's just say the majority of my audience is usually adults. You doing anything tonight? Why don't you come? I've got two front-row seats that were meant for some friends, but something came up, and they can't come."

"Really? Well, yeah, I think I'd enjoy that. Thank you," Dale said happily.

Jack pointed to a napkin. "I left my phone at the hotel, but just write your name on a napkin, and I'll give it to the ticket booth workers. The tickets will be waiting for you at 8 p.m. tonight."

* * *

At 7:30, Dale was out front of Liz and Greg's house, honking the horn. Greg came bounding out of the house. He opened the car door and flopped into the passenger seat somewhat out of breath.

Dale laughed. "Long day?"

"You could say that," Greg said as he put his seat belt on. "I had to get out of the house quickly or it wasn't going to happen. The boys were trying to rope me into taking them to a friend's house."

"Oh yeah?" Dale said as he put the car in drive.

Greg nodded. "Luckily, Liz is working from home. She'll drive them later if she feels like it. The boys just don't want to wait for her to be done."

"OK, I get it now," Dale said with a smirk.

Greg took a deep breath. "So, a magic show, eh? Sounds interesting."

Dale made a left out of the driveway, heading towards downtown Cape May. "Yeah. Have you heard of this guy? Jack Jeffries?"

"You bet. The guy is famous. I've seen a couple episodes of his show. So what's Donna doing? She didn't want to come?" Greg asked.

Dale shook his head. "No, she's working on some seating cards for the wedding, and wasn't feeling up to it. She actually told me to ask you."

"That was nice of her," Greg said, feeling his stomach rumble. "I hope they have snacks at this event. I didn't have time to eat dinner yet."

Ten minutes later, Dale pulled into Cape May Movie Theater's parking lot, and they walked to the ticket booth.

They picked up their tickets and walked through the old lobby, smelling the buttery popcorn at the concession stand and hearing it pop.

"I'm getting popcorn and a soda. You want anything?" Greg asked as he got in line and took out his wallet.

Dale eyed up the glass case full of different candy on display. "I'll take some Sno-Caps."

"It's on me," Greg said when he saw Dale reach for his wallet in his back pocket.

Five minutes later, they were inside the sold-out theater, walking down to the front row where their seats were.

"Jeez Louise. You didn't tell me the tickets were front row," Greg said, feeling surprised. "I don't think I've ever had seats this good."

Dale laughed as he looked up at the big red velvet curtains on the stage before them. "Man, Dave and that crew really did an amazing job bringing this theater back to life. It's great to see them selling the theater out."

Just then, the lights dimmed and red uplights turned on around the entire theater. The orchestra started playing from the pit, and a spotlight was directed on the curtains as they rose, revealing a table with a few objects on it.

As everyone watched in silence, out came Jack Jeffries in a tuxedo to the front of the stage, bowing as he received a standing ovation and screams from the crowd.

Dale and Greg stood up and clapped with everyone else, and then eventually sat down as the music cut off.

Jack started his routine with his beautiful assistant—who was also his wife, Tracy—by having her wheeled out on scaffolding. She stood at the top of the scaffolding, waving to the audience as Jack looked over at her before climbing the scaffolding to be next to her. There, Tracy covered Jack with a tarp, then proceeded to climb down the scaffolding and walk to the front of the stage where a large box stood. She stepped inside of the box.

The orchestra began playing again, and the audience waited in anticipation. Within moments, the tarp was lifted off Jack, revealing it was Tracy under the tarp, and out of the box, stepped Jack.

"What?!" Greg yelled out. "How did they pull that off?"

The audience clapped and cheered, fully stunned at the magic trick they'd just witnessed.

Dale shook his head in disbelief. "I'm thoroughly impressed. Whatever illusion he used, it worked."

Greg shoved a handful of hot popcorn in his mouth as he sat on the edge of his seat, ready for the next magic trick. "Thank you for inviting me. This is what I call entertainment."

"I'll say," Dale said as he tossed some chocolate Sno-Caps in his mouth.

Two hours, and many impressive magic tricks later, the show was over, and everyone filed out of the theater.

Greg pointed to a table by the doors where Jack and Tracy stood signing autographs and greeting the audience. "There he is."

Dale's eyes widened. "There isn't a line yet. Let's go over there now," he said hurrying over as Greg followed behind.

A smile appeared on Jack's face when he saw Dale. "Did you like your first magic show, Dale?"

Dale laughed. "Man, that was incredible. Absolutely mind-blowing. This is my friend, Greg," Dale said pointing.

"Nice to meet you, Jack," Greg said while shaking Jack's hand.

"This is my wife and assistant, Tracy," Jack said putting his arm around Tracy's shoulders.

Dale and Greg both smiled and nodded at her. "Pleased to meet you."

Dale stuffed his hands into his pockets. "I just wanted to say thank you so much for the tickets, Jack. If you're in town again, stop by my restaurant. Lunch and dinner are on me. Heck, come stay at my house if you want," Dale said half-jokingly.

Greg chuckled. "Don't mind Dale. He's extra amped from that amazing show. He's also getting married on July 4."

Tracy's eyes widened. "Married on July 4? Look at that, honey, we're going to be here that week for vacation."

Jack nodded. "We kind of fell in love with Cape May the last couple of days and found a cancellation at a hotel for Fourth of July week. If you want a little magic show for the guests, let me know."

"You're kidding!" Dale said, his face flushing with excitement.

"I'm not. Here, put my number in your phone and give me a call," Jack said as Dale fumbled with his phone.

Greg laughed as Dale plugged the number into his contacts. "You just made Dale's night. You don't even know."

Jack smiled as he noticed a super long line forming behind Greg and Dale. "I do what I can. Plus, Tracy over here always wanted a Fourth of July wedding. I think she'd love to be there," he said as they leaned in for a kiss.

Dale shook Jack's then Tracy's hand. "We'll talk soon. Again, fantastic show. Absolutely incredible," he said as he and Greg walked out of the theater and under the brightly lit marquis.

CHAPTER THREE

Liz pulled up in her car five minutes early to the front of one of the biggest and most glamorous Victorians in Cape May. Ocean Dust was a residence unlike most of the other Victorians around it that had been made into bed-and-breakfasts over the years. The outside was painted navy blue and the trim was painted pink, clashing perfectly against each other. A wooden arch covered with pink roses stood at the foot of the walkway. It was easily worth a few million or more.

"Well, I just pulled up. I'm so excited I can barely take it," Liz said into her speaker phone.

"You're going to kill it. Knock their socks off," Greg said over loud kitchen noises.

"What's going on at the restaurant today?" Liz asked curiously. "I can hear the commotion."

Greg tasted the chicken picante dish in front of him, then looked over at the cooks and gave them a thumbs-up. "We decided to come in on our day off to perfect the new menu items. So far so good. I really think these new entrees are going to be a hit."

Liz smiled. "Well, make sure you keep some of the customer favorites. You don't want to upset anybody."

"Oh, for sure. Our most popular dishes are staying," Greg said.

Liz looked back at the house, noticing not a single car was in the driveway. "I'm so nervous. This will be my biggest interior design client yet. We agreed on a price, and let's just say I'll be making double what I did last year. We're finally meeting today after weeks of phone calls discussing everything."

A loud crash of plates could be heard behind Greg then some yelling. "Oh jeez. Guys! We just got those plates in. Try to be more careful," Greg yelled over the commotion.

"Alright, well, I'll let you go. I have to go meet the owners now," Liz said, looking at the clock.

"Call me when you're done. I can't wait to hear how it went," Greg said enthusiastically.

Liz hung up the phone and got out of the car, smoothing her skirt and blouse. She had dressed to the nines for the meeting and even had on her expensive heels that she only wore to special events. Presentation was everything, especially for an interior designer.

As she approached the house, she noticed all the shades were shut and curtains were drawn. Not a single light appeared to be on though it was in the middle of the day. She knocked on the door and waited while fidgeting with her tablet and purse.

Thirty seconds passed and nothing. She knocked again. And again. It appeared nobody was home. Liz stepped back to make sure she was at the right home, checking the house number with her notes. She was indeed at the right place.

"I guess they forgot about our meeting," Liz said to herself as she pulled her cell phone out of her purse to call Natasha, the owner she'd been dealing with.

Natasha's husband gave her the reins, letting her handle it all, so he hadn't been involved. The call immediately went to voicemail. "Hi, Natasha. It's Liz. I'm here at the house for our nine o'clock meeting. Give me a call back," Liz said as she hung up and headed back to the car.

Liz got in the car, sighed deeply, and leaned her head back on the headrest. She then called Greg back.

"That was quick," Greg said, sautéing sounds filling the background.

Liz shrugged. "They're not home, and Natasha, the owner, is not answering my call, which is unlike her. I'm wondering if they went out somewhere and forgot about our meeting."

Greg shifted his eyes. "Weren't you just talking to her last night?"

Liz nodded. "Yes, I was. You know what … I thought about waiting here to see if they come back in the next ten minutes, but I have some errands I need to run. I'm sure they'll call later, and we'll reschedule."

"Sounds good. Oh yeah, all this food we're cooking and trying out here? There'll be plenty to bring home, so I'll take care of dinner," Greg said.

"You're the best," Liz said as she hung up and put the car into drive.

In the grocery store, '90s easy listening music played over the speakers as she plopped the boys' favorite boxes of cereal into the cart when a text notification chimed on her phone.

Liz glanced at it, noticing it was from Natasha. She stopped in her tracks and read the text.

Hi Liz. I got your voice message. We've decided to go with a different interior designer. Best wishes.

Liz stood staring at her phone in disbelief.

"Excuse me," a voice said behind Liz.

Liz looked up from her phone, not realizing her cart was in the middle of the aisle, making it impossible for anyone to pass her. "Sorry about that," she said as she moved her cart to the side, still looking at her phone in complete shock.

She immediately called Greg again. She needed to discuss this with someone immediately before she had a meltdown.

"Hey, hon," Greg said happily.

Liz got right to the point. "Greg, Natasha just sent me a text message saying they've decided to go with a different interior designer."

Greg's heart sank. "What? Why? Did they say why they weren't at the house to meet you?"

Liz shook her head. "No, and not even an apology for wasting my time today. I feel sick to my stomach," Liz said, her hand shaking as she held her phone.

Greg bit his lip. "Maybe call her back and see why they've opted to go with someone else?"

Liz felt tears welling up in her eyes. "Greg, I did call them. She even said that she got my voicemail in the text message. She opted to text me back and not call. Obviously, they're avoiding me both in person and on the phone. I'm not calling her. The income from this project was important. I've been struggling financially with this business lately, and I just don't know what to do anymore. I feel completely gutted," Liz said, the tears now starting to trickle down her cheek.

Greg nodded in agreement, his heart in pieces for Liz. "Look, I'm not going to be home for a few hours. Go for a walk and clear your head. Maybe call a friend. We can discuss it more when I get home. Try not to let it bother you too much," Greg said with concern.

Liz took a deep breath and composed herself. "You're right. I'm at ACME getting a few things, but I think I do need to go do something."

"Good. By the way, are you going to text Natasha back?" Greg asked hesitantly.

Liz rolled her eyes at the thought of talking to Natasha again. "I thought about it. I'm not sure if I should or not. She surely took the coward's way out here, and I can't really respect that. I don't think it will be worth my time."

Greg sighed. "Well, at least tonight we'll have a wonderful

feast of a meal. I think you and the boys are going to love it. I'm even bringing some dessert."

Liz mustered a smile. "You are the best, Greg. What would I ever do without you?"

* * *

Blocks away, the Book Nook was busier than ever.

With a white towel over her shoulder, Sarah handed a customer their iced coffee as Erin, one of her shop employees, took the orders. The line grew longer and longer, and Sarah blinked her eyes in amazement, watching the line circle all the way out the door.

"OK, I'm back from lunch," Bert, another Book Nook employee, said as he put on his apron and stepped behind the counter.

Sarah sighed with relief. "Great, you've got it from here?"

Bert smiled. "I'll have this line gone in minutes. I'm the fastest barista around these parts. Best, too," he said confidently.

Erin nudged Bert. "He's not lying. I've seen it."

Bert blushed and smiled at Erin.

Sarah nodded, taking off her apron and setting the towel down. "You're the greatest, you two. I'm going to go see how the class is going," she said as she walked to another area of the shop.

There, among the tall rows of bookshelves as well as couches and chairs where customers read and relaxed, was a long table off to the side full of people taking part in a terrarium-making class. It wasn't exactly the best place to hold the class as it was right in front of bookshelves that customers may have needed to get to, but it was the only spot available that was big enough for the class of fifteen people, even if they were squished in.

"OK, everyone, now take your succulents and place them

in the soil inside of your glass terrarium just like this," Cindy, the class instructor, said as she demonstrated on her own terrarium. "Isn't this great? Imagine this sitting in your kitchen window. I mean, it's perfect." Cindy was fifty years old with bright-pink hair and wore cat-eye glasses, and she was one of the most enthusiastic people Sarah had ever met. She was the perfect person to run a class, which is why Sarah loved the idea of having it hosted at the Book Nook. Business-wise, it brought more people into the bookshop, and it added a little excitement to the normally quiet store.

"How's everything going?" Sarah asked Cindy.

Cindy held out her hand. "See for yourself. Don't the terrariums look lovely?" The students held up their terrariums, proudly showcasing what they had done.

"Wow. Looks great!" Sarah said with a big smile.

Sarah watched as two customers tried to scoot behind the table to get a book in the romance section, which was blocked by the class. "So sorry. Can you two get back there OK?" Sarah asked.

Cindy spoke up. "We can push our chairs in, right guys?"

Everyone nodded and scooched in closer to the table, which helped a little bit but not much.

Just then, Sarah heard a familiar voice next to her. "Hey, girl. What's going on here?" Sarah looked over to see Liz sipping a coffee and pointing at the terrariums.

Sarah smiled. "Liz, what are you doing here? I thought you were out with some clients."

Liz rolled her eyes. "I just had the biggest potential client of my life cancel our entire project today. I'm taking Greg's advice and clearing my head. I figured starting with a coffee at a friend's shop was a good way to kick that off."

Sarah scratched her head. "Are you serious? What happened?"

Liz shrugged. "Beats me. I know as much as you. I didn't

even get a phone call. Just a short text message. It royally sucks."

Sarah shook her head. "I'm so sorry. I know you'll find something better. Maybe an even bigger client."

Liz took a sip of coffee. "I don't know about that. It's been getting harder and harder to find clients lately. I'm getting a little stressed honestly. Anyway ... back to this," she said pointing at the table of students. "What's going on?"

Sarah looked up the stairs. "Wanna go upstairs and talk?"

"Sure," Liz said as she followed Sarah up the creaky wooden steps to a beautiful room full of more books and some seats. Sunlight poured through a stained-glass window amongst the dim lamp lighting.

They both sat down on the couch together, and Liz started flipping through the coffee table book full of different horse breeds before putting it down, giving Sarah her full attention.

Sarah cleared her throat. "So, I've been trying out something new. Running different classes and group discussions here."

"Yeah, I've noticed. Are you getting a small cut from the class?" Liz asked.

Sarah shook her head. "I'm not. The people running the classes are not making a huge profit from them since they have to purchase the supplies and give their time teaching the class. Really, having these classes is bringing the Book Nook more business as the students tend to buy drinks and purchase books afterwards. Not only that, but it's making this place livelier. I actually love it."

"That's really neat," Liz said as she eyed the vintage wooden coffee table in front of them.

Sarah nodded. "The only issue is I'm running out of room, and I don't have a good spot to host these classes. As it stands today, the class is blocking some bookshelves, and even though I like that it's lively, I feel like some people might find it awkward to shop while a whole class is going on next to them. I have to figure something out."

"Well, what about hosting it up here?" Liz asked.

Sarah stroked her chin. "It's cramped and the air-conditioning doesn't work well up here. It gets way too hot in the summer. Maybe in the winter, but I'm not thinking that far ahead yet."

Liz bit her lip as she ran her hand over the coffee table. "Not to change the subject, but I just realized this is the coffee table I refurbished. I forgot I gave this to you."

"Yes, you did such a good job. We didn't have room for it at the house, so I found the perfect place for it here. Have you thought about getting back into doing that?" Sarah asked.

Liz paused for a moment. "Nope. I got way too busy with my interior design job. Between that, the boys' hectic schedules, and running the Seahorse Inn, I haven't had a lick of time for hobbies lately."

Sarah stood up and led the way back down the stairs with Liz following behind. "Well, I know this client cancelling is not the greatest, but maybe it'll force you to have more time for yourself for a bit? Look at the silver lining?"

Liz sighed and nodded. "I knew coming here would make me feel better."

Sarah put her arm around Liz's shoulders as they walked through the shelves of books, passing people reading while drinking their coffees, teas, and eating their pastries.

Suddenly, loud laughing came from the class in the corner, causing Sarah to sharply turn her head in that direction, as well as everyone else in the store.

Cindy laughed with the table of students as they tried to place little gnomes, deer, and mushroom figurines throughout their terrariums. Nobody's hand seemed small enough to get it done right as the gnomes would only lay down in the dirt and the deer and mushrooms ended up inside the succulents.

"I think tweezers are in order next time," Cindy said as she tried to help some of the students get the figurines placed correctly.

The table of students loudly laughed again, causing it to echo from wall to wall, and Sarah and Liz both noticed annoyed looks on some customers' faces as they picked up their drinks and books and left the room in a hurry.

CHAPTER FOUR

Dave rubbed his hands over his face, then looked up at the canopy of trees above him at Fox Run Wildlife Refuge. He smelled the forest fire and saw the foggy haze of smoke, even if it was miles away at this point.

A truck pulled up, and guy in overalls with a bushy red beard jumped out and walked to the back. He looked around, trying to find anyone, when he spotted Dave. "Hey. Mind helping me a moment?"

Dave nodded and headed over, even though he was in the middle of something. As he approached the truck and the man opened the tailgate, he saw two sickly fawns, and his heart sank.

The guy leaned on the truck, staring at them. "They must have gotten separated from their mother. They're covered in ticks from head and toe and seem very hungry. They're skinny as rails."

Dave's eyes softened. He knew they definitely hadn't been with their mom in a while as those ticks would have been groomed off by her. "This is only my third day here. I came up to help out from Cape May. Let me run inside and see where they can put these little guys," Dave said as he hurried into the wildlife hospital.

Once inside, it was nothing but chaos. Usually, the wild animals were put into kennels in the back where it was quiet and away from visitors, but due to being overcrowded from the fires, there were cages and crates lined up all the way out in the lobby and even in the laundry room, kitchen, and basement.

Julie, the wildlife hospital manager, ran feverishly around the hospital, checking up on the volunteers, then stopped when she saw Dave. "Is everything OK out there?"

Dave sighed. "We've got two orphaned fawns in a guy's truck. Just seeing where they could possibly go."

Julie held her face with her hands, feeling completely overwhelmed. "We just had two kennels open up in the back. I know you're busy outside, but do you mind bringing them in?"

Dave nodded. "No problem at all," he said as he headed out to the truck and told the guy what they were doing.

Minutes later, both Dave and the man each held a crying, hungry fawn, placing them into kennels. The man went to the front desk and filled out an intake form while Dave watched as a volunteer pulled one of the fawns out to assess it.

"You're hungry, aren't you," the volunteer said as she felt its skinny little body. "You're also covered in ticks. Let's get you hydrated and fed, and then we'll get these bloodsuckers off."

Dave smiled, feeling more optimistic about the fawn's chances now. "I'm heading back out. Let me know if you need anything," he said as he walked outside just as the man was leaving in his truck.

Once outside, Dave heard banging noises around the refuge. It sounded like a construction zone. He walked over to where he'd left his hammer and headed over to the team of volunteers he was leading.

"How's it going over here?" Dave asked as he watched three guys place a roof on top of a large fenced-in enclosure.

"It's going great. This enclosure will fit eight of the adult raccoons comfortably until they're well enough to be released,"

Don, one of the volunteers, said. "This should free up some room in the hospital."

Dave nodded. "You guys are really good at this. They asked me to come in and help lead these projects, but you all know what you're doing."

Trent, another volunteer, sighed. "Thank you for the compliment, but we're glad you're here. Any help is appreciated. Not to mention, you're quicker than all of us. Since you got here Saturday, you've put together five of these enclosures. This is only our second one," he said with a laugh.

Dave shrugged and smiled. "I have an advantage since I've been doing this for many years, I guess. Also, seeing all these animals in need has really boosted my stamina."

* * *

Back in Cape May, Margaret was outside pruning the tomatoes in the vegetable garden. They had made the garden plots twice as big as last year's and therefore planted twice as much, vastly surpassing the garden they had planted on Liz and Greg's property.

There were over fifty varieties of tomatoes, both heirlooms and hybrids. Then there was the huge patch of onions, summer squash and zucchini, lima beans, eggplant, peppers, watermelon and cantaloupe, winter squash, and everything in between.

As Margaret clipped off a large sucker on a tall tomato plant, some movement across the way caught her eye. She turned her head to see her neighbor again. This time, he was filling up his birdbath with water from a watering can.

Margaret stood up and, without a second thought, walked over to him, waving her hands in the air. "Hi!" she yelled out.

The neighbor glanced up from filling the birdbath and gave a little nod and smile. Margaret took that as her cue to continue all the way over to meet him once and for all.

As Margaret approached, she pulled off her gardening gloves and put her hand out for a handshake. "I'm Margaret," she said somewhat out of breath from the quick trek across the yard.

"I'm Frank," the neighbor said as he set the watering can down on the ground.

"I'm so sorry we haven't met before now. We tried a few times to no avail," Margaret said as she looked around his well-manicured yard.

Frank nodded. "Well, I didn't make it easy for you. My beloved wife, Doris, passed six months ago. Before that, she was in a nursing home for a year, as I wasn't able to care for her like she needed. I spent every day with her there, only returning in the evenings to sleep."

Margaret felt her heart sink. "I'm so sorry to hear about your loss. I know that must be difficult for you."

Frank looked down at the ground. "It was hard, but it was also rough before she passed. She had Alzheimer's so she didn't even know who I was for a good while."

Margaret shook her head. "So sorry to hear that. My husband, Dave, and our girls, Harper and Abby, would be glad to help you with anything you need anytime."

Frank sighed. "You're too kind. Thank you for that. You know, we've lived here for around sixty years. Doris and I were the original owners of this house. Your house, though, is much older. It has a lot more history, and an interesting history at that."

Margaret widened her eyes in curiosity and shock. "I knew our property was once a farm, but that's the extent of it. We'll have to come visit or have you over to hear about that. We'd be interested to know more about our land and this overall area."

Frank nodded as he hunched down slowly to pick up the watering can while pointing towards Margaret and Dave's yard. "I've noticed you have some big gardens over there. When we were raising our kids, I had a job working on the farm right there on your property. It might be why I might know a thing or two," he said with a little smile.

* * *

The sun shined brightly on the water as Chris sighed happily while standing on the dock looking at his stunning new birding boat.

"She's a beaut," a voice said next to him.

Chris looked over to see Dale standing cross-armed next to him. "Well, if it isn't the soon-to-be groom himself," Chris said as he gave Dale a back pat and a hug.

Dale nodded happily. "Yeah, I figured I'd stop by and say hi on my way to work. Can you believe the big day is next week? I can't."

Chris shook his head in disbelief. "It seems like yesterday that you proposed."

"It definitely does. So, you got a new boat?" Dale asked as he nodded towards it.

Chris uncrossed his arms. "Yep. I was selling out birding tours every day last year, and I figured I'd bring a second boat on."

"That's great," Dale said, eyeing the boat up. "Did you hire an extra captain?"

"I did. His name is Eric. Younger guy. I want say late twenties, but he used to run a boating business with his dad over in Stone Harbor for about ten years. He's got a good amount of experience and appears to be pretty responsible, though he does have that younger mentality still. Did you want to see the new boat?"

"Let's do it," Dale said as he led the way towards the ramp. The new boat was a huge upgrade from Chris's older one. Everything was newer and nicer, right down to the seating.

"I'll be driving the new boat, and Eric will be in charge of the older boat. We'll be running both simultaneously,"

Chris said as he ran his hand over the shiny silver steering wheel.

"That sounds like a good plan," Dale said as they headed back to the dock, passing a row of paddleboards on the way. "These yours too?" Dale asked.

Chris knocked on one of the boards. "Yes, I'm also offering paddleboarding out here in addition to the kayaking tours. I've got someone lined up to do some paddleboard yoga classes through the next couple of months too."

Dale smiled. "That's really cool, Chris. Proud of you, man. I gotta get going. I'll give you a call soon."

* * *

Lisa parked her lime-green vintage VW Bus on a short dead-end road near a secluded beach, which was only well-known to the locals due to the location being away from the hubbub of town. She followed a narrow sandy beach path bordered by coastal pines and spruces. The end of the path led to small bright-green house with white lace curtains in the windows.

A woman stood at the front door looking at her phone, before she noticed Lisa approaching. "Hi! Are you Lisa?"

Lisa nodded and smiled. "I am! And you're Carrie?"

"That's me. Normally I hire a realtor to take care of showing our rentals, but they all seem to be on vacation this week," she said with a slight chuckle. "Come inside and see our place," she said opening the door.

Lisa stepped into the house first and immediately was smitten. The inside was, in one word, adorable. It was completely furnished and had a wonderfully quaint and cozy feeling to it. The walls were painted white with a blue-and-white gingham couch in the living room. Above the couch were framed hand-made crewels of different potted flowers. The kitchen had a variety of different teakettles lining a shelf above the sink, and the bedroom had a queen bed, dresser, and the perfect little nook with a window where a desk had been placed to overlook the small backyard.

"My husband and I take a lot of pride in this little place. It was our first house together. I loved this location so much that a part of me wanted to tear it down and build our bigger home here, but we couldn't bear to do it. It's too sentimental to us," Carrie said as she fixed a peach-colored throw blanket on the back of the chair she was standing next to.

Lisa smiled. "I can see why you wanted to keep it as is. It has so much charm."

Carrie nodded. "So, what do you think? Interested in renting it?"

Lisa took one more glance towards the kitchen, noticing the strawberry tea towels draped over the oven door handle. It was so charming and inviting. "Yes, I definitely am. Are you still OK with a month-to-month lease? I'm newly divorced and just left Hawaii. So, I'm starting fresh back in my hometown for a bit."

Carrie sighed. "Girl, I know all about starting over from a divorce. My sister rented this place after her divorce, and she loved it. You'll fall in love with Cape May again, and who knows, maybe find yourself a hot local man too," she said with a chuckle.

Lisa smiled as she looked up, noticing a ceiling fan. "Well, that's sort of already happened."

Suddenly Carrie felt as though she was talking to an old friend. "You're kidding," she said, smacking Lisa on the shoulder.

Lisa shrugged. "Met him at Joe's Oyster Bar. His name is Nick. Turns out we had crushes on each other one summer as teenagers."

Carrie opened her mouth in disbelief. "Nick? From Joe's Oyster Bar? You're kidding. I know him."

Lisa bit her lip. "You know him?"

Carrie shifted her eyes. "Well, I'm not sure if I should

mention this, but he did date my sister for a little bit after her divorce … while she was living here actually."

"Oh …" Lisa said awkwardly, not sure of how to take that information.

Carrie sighed. "Oh jeez. Why did I say that? You probably don't need to know all that."

"No, it's OK. I mean we all date people throughout our lives, right?" Lisa said with a smile. "Nick and I are still getting to know each other, so I don't know too much about his dating history yet. We're just taking it slow."

"Slow?" Carrie asked with shock on her face.

"Why do you ask it like that?" Lisa asked, confused.

Carrie shook her head. "You know what. I think I've said too much. Why don't we end that topic here."

Lisa nodded, but deep down, she wanted to know what Carrie was getting at. Why was it such a surprise that she and Nick were taking things slow?

Carrie led the way out of the house, and after locking up, they stood outside. "So, I'll send you the lease tonight. Then, I'll just need first month, last month, and a security deposit. Does that work?"

"Works great," Lisa said as she turned towards the ocean, hearing the faint sound of waves in the distance.

"You're going to love living here. It's so quiet and dark at night. You can see all the stars on a clear evening, and it's just magical. On a nice day, open the windows and take in the scent of the pines and ocean," Carrie said as she took a breath, remembering her happy younger days of living there with her husband.

Lisa smiled and thanked Carrie, then headed back down the narrow beach path to her van. She was so excited to land such a neat place, but at the same time, she had a sinking feeling in her stomach. Carrie seemed to know something about Nick that Lisa didn't, but why would she avoid the topic?

CHAPTER FIVE

Donna walked around Dale and Donna's Funnel Cakes shop on Wildwood Boardwalk, wiping down dirty tables, which immediately were filled in with new people looking for a space to eat their piping-hot funnel cakes. She then headed over to the counter where her employees were busy taking orders and making funnel cakes.

"Are you doing OK over here, Chelsea?" Donna asked the employee who was taking the orders.

Chelsea looked over at Pete as he sprinkled powdered sugar over an order. "Yeah, we've got a nice little system going. Pete is killing it back there."

Pete smiled at Chelsea. "Ah, shucks."

Donna sighed with relief. "Great. I think I'm going to get out of here."

Chelsea nodded as she handed a customer his change. "We can handle it. Don't worry."

"You're the best," Donna said as she grabbed her stuff and stepped out of the air-conditioned shop and onto the hot boardwalk.

The seagulls circled and squawked high above, and lots of people were only in bathing suits and flip-flops while walking the boards. She watched as two girls in their twenties passed by in clothes Donna wore in the '90s. It made her smile, but it also gave her the urge to get back in a thrift store because it'd been many months since she'd been in one. She picked up her phone and called Liz.

"Hey!" Liz yelled into the phone, picking it up on the first ring.

"Did I call at a bad time?" Donna asked.

Liz sat in her office staring at a blank screen. "No, you called at a perfect time. I've got nothing to do."

Donna shifted her eyes. "Nothing? You're not working?"

Liz shook her head. "I guess I haven't told you yet. The other day, the biggest client I've ever had cancelled on me. That project was going to be a game changer for my business. Since I set aside months to work on it and turned down other projects, I'm now sitting here twiddling my thumbs, staring at my computer screen, hoping another project comes through … But who am I kidding? It's the slowest time of the year for me. Everyone is taking their summer vacation. What about you? What's going on?"

Donna nodded. "I just got off work. I'm about to head home and got the urge to go thrifting. Why don't I pick you up, we'll grab iced coffees and go scavenging for treasures?"

"Say no more. You had me at iced coffee," Liz said as she slammed her laptop shut and popped out of her seat, sliding her feet into her shoes in the process. "I'll be ready when you get here."

Twenty minutes later, Donna pulled up in front of Liz's house and honked. Liz came out of the house, hopped into the car, and noticed the iced coffees in the cup holders. "You already picked them up?"

Donna nodded and smiled. "Yes, I figured I'd grab them on the boardwalk before I headed over," Donna said as she put the car in drive and drove towards her favorite thrift store.

Thirty minutes later, they arrived at the absolutely huge

store. It looked to be housed in an old grocery store with racks and racks of clothing everywhere. Off to the side were many hard goods, books, electronics, and furniture.

"I'm going to look at the clothes," Donna said.

Liz scanned the thrift store, her eye catching on something in the corner. "I'm heading over there," she said, pointing to a back room across the store.

Liz got to the back room filled with old furniture. Most of it was cheap junk, but there, hiding in plain sight, was a mid-century modern bedroom set containing a dresser and two end tables.

Liz's eyes widened in disbelief as she looked at the price. Only one-hundred dollars for the set, but she'd started to see why. There was a ton of damage to the tops of the furniture—lots of scratches and water marks. She paused for a moment, stepping back to get a better look at it.

Years ago, she refurbished pieces like this easily; but now, how would she have time with her business? That was … assuming business picked up. Then again, where would she do it at the house? She would need a large space that could get messy. She'd need good sanders and stains, and a circular saw. Suddenly, the thought of taking on these kind of projects seemed way too overwhelming. She decided she should get Donna's thoughts on the matter, so she trekked across the store towards the clothing, but Donna wasn't anywhere in sight.

"Donna?" Liz softly yelled over some clothing racks as she walked around. There wasn't an answer. "Donna?" Liz yelled louder.

This time, a muffled voice could be heard from the dressing room.

Liz headed that way, this time calling out again, "Donna?"

"Liz? Is that you?" Donna asked from inside the dressing room.

Liz nodded as she looked down at Donna's feet under the

dressing room door, noticing her friend was dancing. "I need your opinion on something over there."

Donna laughed happily. "Well, I need yours. How about I come out and you tell me," Donna said as she slowly opened the dressing room door, revealing herself.

Liz's mouth dropped open. "Wow!"

Donna smiled big as she looked at Liz, then nodded happily at some nearby shoppers who stopped to admire her. She wore the most gorgeous vintage Gunne Sax wedding gown. It was off the shoulder, long and free-flowing, simple yet elegant. It was white with baby-blue trim pieces and lace, and it fit Donna like a glove. "Weeks of looking for a wedding dress, and I've found the *one*," Donna said as she looked at herself in the mirror.

Liz laughed with excitement. "That dress was made for you. It fits you perfectly too."

"That's what's crazy about this. I didn't have much time to get anything altered, and then I find this dress. It's only fifteen dollars. Can you believe it?" Donna asked, feeling on cloud nine with the best thrift find of her life.

"This dress was meant for you," Liz said, smiling.

Donna nodded as she walked back into the dressing room. "Finally, something that makes me feel like *me*. It even comes with the original dress bag to protect it. I'm taking this off, and then you show me what you're looking at over across the store."

Five minutes later, Liz was back in front of the vintage dresser set with Donna. "You know how I used to refurbish furniture? Sarah put it in my head that I should maybe give it a try again. I sold a few pieces many years ago, but mainly I did it for myself or for friends and family. I'd have to get a bunch of supplies to do it again *and* find a space somewhere, but do you think I should buy it? Is it really a good idea to get back into it?"

Donna nodded enthusiastically while holding her dress.

"Yes, you should buy it. Maybe we can get the guys to help load it into Dale's truck. Then, you can work your magic."

Liz sighed, feeling a sense of relief and dread at the same time. "Sarah was trying to talk me into doing it again, and now you're all for it. I guess I should do it. It's not like I have any big interior design projects to work on at the moment."

Donna rested her arm on Liz's shoulder. "You need something new but also familiar to keep your mind occupied right now while you figure out your interior design business. I think this is it. Plus, I could use a few pieces for our place," she said with a wink.

Liz ran her hand over the dresser and a rush of excitement that she hadn't experienced in a while coursed through her body. She decided in that moment she was ready to use her interior design eye and past refurbishing experience to dive headfirst into this project.

* * *

An hour later, Donna and Liz drove back from the thrift store followed by Greg, Dale, and Liz and Greg's sons, Michael and Steven, in Dale's truck.

Donna looked in her rearview mirror at the guys laughing and talking in the truck with the strapped-in furniture piled high in the back. "Looks like they're having a ball back there."

Liz laughed. "Those two men together are a hoot. Throw in our boys and I'm sure it's even more fun."

Donna nodded and glanced at Liz. "Did Greg tell you about the magic show they went to?"

"He did. Jack Jeffries, right? He was pretty impressed. We've seen his TV show a handful of times, but Greg said seeing him in person was completely different. Better, in fact," Liz said.

Donna chuckled. "Dale went from never having seen a magic show and not knowing much about it to being so enthralled with it that it's all he talks about now. Since that show, he's bought books on magicians, watched videos online, joined social media groups revolving around the topic. He's hyper fixated on it for sure. I don't know how he got Jack Jeffries to agree to perform at our wedding—"

Liz dropped her jaw in shock. "You're kidding. I hadn't heard that part yet. How do you feel about all of this?"

Donna shrugged. "I love seeing him so interested in new things … but I have to say, I've never been into magicians. As a kid, they always seemed so hokey. It's not really my thing, but I'm willing to have a little magic show for the wedding guests. I think it would be fun for everyone. Oh, by the way, we're keeping it a surprise for the guests. I only brought it up to you because I figured Greg had said something already."

Liz nodded. "My lips are sealed. Gosh, I can't believe the wedding is next week already."

Donna shook her head in amazement. "You're telling me. I can't believe I just now found my wedding dress with the wedding being next week."

Liz laughed. "Well, you always were a procrastinator growing up."

Donna nodded in agreement. "I was, wasn't I? It always seemed to work out even better when I waited until the last minute for some reason. Maybe I knew that deep down when I started looking for wedding dresses."

* * *

It was early afternoon, and Judy was starting her first beach-tag checker shift, filling in for someone who had to leave early. Judy found a parking spot blocks away and lugged her beach chair and umbrella toward the Coral Avenue beach entrance in Cape May Point. She finally got to the path and stopped for a minute to catch her breath. The sun was hot, and the air was thick, and there wasn't anything close to a breeze.

Judy wiped the sweat off her forehead with the back of her arm, then trekked up the beach path until she saw Angela, a seventy-year-old woman who looked like she never missed a workout, sitting there in her chair under an umbrella with perfect hair and makeup, awaiting the beachgoers coming onto the beach.

"Hi, you must be Judy," Angela said as she got up to shake Judy's hand with her beautifully manicured nails.

Judy nodded as she caught her breath, trying to sneak in some oxygen through the thick air, while shaking Angela's hand "And you must be Angela. Nice to meet you. This is my first day filling in."

Angela started packing up her umbrella and chair. "Oh, you'll do great. I'll leave you with the beach tags and the credit card device. I hope you brought a good book."

Judy looked into her purse, realizing she had totally forgotten to bring one. "Well, I don't think I did. I'll figure out a way to keep my mind occupied," she said as she let her chair and umbrella fall onto the hot sand.

Angela noticed the sweat pouring from Judy's face and immediately felt the need to offer a hand. "Here, let me help you get situated. I'll get the umbrella in the sand for you."

Judy smiled with relief. "Thanks, you're a doll. So, you enjoy being a beach tag checker?"

Angela screwed the large umbrella anchor into the sand and then opened the umbrella up, which gave a lot of shade for Judy's chair. "I do. I love it. I've always been a beach gal, though. It's one of my favorite things to do. If you like the beach, you'll enjoy it. Well, I'd better be going. You're filling in for me as I have an appointment to get to. I can't thank you enough."

Judy plopped into her chair as Angela handed her the bag of beach tags, which she promptly put in her fanny pack. The mobile card reader, she stuck in the cup holder of the chair.

"Good luck, Angela," Judy said as Angela walked effortlessly back down the beach path.

Judy had finally relaxed and was cooling off under the umbrella when she heard a commotion down by the water. She stood up to get a better look, noticing people were pointing at the ocean. She couldn't see what they were all looking at, so she walked towards a couple about ten feet away.

"What's everyone staring at?" Judy asked the couple.

"There's a whole pod of dolphins out there. There're a couple that are putting on quite a show, jumping pretty high out of the water," the woman said.

"You're kidding," Judy said with excitement.

Just then, the crowd of people on the beach let out oohs and aahs as the dolphin pod reappeared, putting on another spectacular jumping show. Judy couldn't keep her eyes off them. She'd never in her life seen dolphins do anything but swim by.

A couple minutes later, she looked over to see a large crowd walking right by her with their beach chairs and umbrellas. They had just walked onto the beach, and she was not at her post to check their beach tags, and more were coming up the path. She scrambled back to her chair just in the nick of time to not miss anyone else.

"Do you have your beach tags?" Judy asked as she greeted the beachgoers. They all nodded and showed their season tags. She felt relieved. At least her first beachgoers were easy.

Moments later, a couple came down the path. They didn't have beach tags and opted to buy two day passes with a credit card.

"Oh jeez. This is my first time using this device," Judy said as she fumbled with the credit card reader, suddenly realizing Angela never showed her how to use it.

The couple smiled politely as they watched Judy take their card and attempt to process the transaction. After multiple failed attempts, she looked up at them. "You don't happen to have cash, do you? I wasn't trained on this device yet."

The man shook his head. "We don't, but we do actually use that device at my job. I can quickly show you how to work it, if that's OK."

Judy sighed with relief. "That would be wonderful. Thank you so much."

CHAPTER SIX

Margaret walked through her raised bed herb garden by the back door, running her hands over the tops of the dill, basil, oregano, and thyme before lifting her hand to her nose to take in the lovely scent that lingered on her skin. She looked over to see Harper and Abby in their bathing suits, swaying on the tire swing that Dave had put up on the old oak tree. Harper sat in the middle of the tire, and Abby sat on top of it, her legs dangling over the front as the tire whipped back and forth. It was really hot out, and it had seemed a month had passed since they'd had any rain.

"Hey, you two. Be careful!" Margaret yelled as she eyed the girls swinging wildly on the tire swing.

The girls didn't hear her but ended up hopping off the tire swing and running towards the sprinkler that Margaret had aimed onto the flower bed. Harper and Abby giggled as they carefully hopped around the zinnias and cosmos until they were smack under the sprinkler getting soaked and enjoying every minute of cooling off from the humid air.

Margaret giggled as she watched them, then started walking towards them when she noticed Frank out in his back-yard again. This time he was waving at Margaret. She waved back, then glanced at the girls who were finished in the sprinkler and now running towards the large raspberry patch to pick a snack.

"Girls, I'm going to talk to our neighbor," Margaret said as she headed towards Frank, but all the while keeping an eye on Harper and Abby.

"Good morning, Frank," Margaret said as she approached him.

Frank looked adorable. He had on a long-sleeved red plaid shirt and suspenders attached to his brown corduroy pants. His outfit was topped off with a newsboy cap and a hoe in his hands.

"Margaret. So glad you're out and about today. I forgot to show you what I've got growing over here," Frank said as he motioned for her to follow him. They slowly headed towards the garage and there, hidden from view on the other side of it, was a small fenced-in raised bed garden.

"Frank, you didn't tell me you had a garden. Did you plant this all on your own?" Margaret asked.

Frank nodded as he proudly looked over his garden. He had pole beans growing up arched cattle panels between beds and a row of sunflowers in the back, and everywhere else was filled in with lush green tomato plants, bright-yellow squash ready for harvest, peppers, eggplants, and more. "My wife and I grew a garden together every year. It was one of our greatest pleasures. It's such a joy to see you and your husband bring the farm next door back to life. Anyway, I forgot to show you this the other day."

Margaret stood stunned at how much work this frail, hunched-over man was able to do with the garden. "It's absolutely gorgeous. I love it," Margaret said as she peered into her yard to make sure the girls were doing OK. "You'll have to meet my husband, Dave, when he gets back. You'll love him. He used to live on a working farm as a kid, and we had a big garden on my sister's property before we bought this house here."

Frank rubbed his chin. "Oh, really? Where is Dave?"

"He's actually up in North Jersey helping a wildlife refuge that's overwhelmed with displaced and hurt wildlife from the forest fires. They're working around the clock up there. I've barely talked to him, aside from maybe five minutes each evening," Margaret said.

Frank smiled. "Sounds like you've got a good one. Distance makes the heart grow fonder, you know. There was one year where I took a job for six months in Utah. Doris stayed back with the kids, and by the time I came back home to my family, I was ready to kiss the ground here. I never took a job away from them again after that, even though I had many appealing opportunities that would have helped us financially."

A crow squawked from inside a large lilac bush, and Frank immediately turned his head to look. "They're back. The crows are back. I can't believe it!" he said with widened eyes.

Margaret bit her lip. "The crows are back?"

Frank clapped his hands. "Yes. They didn't come last year, but the two years before they did. They build their nest high up in the oak tree on your property, and they like to get their twigs from this lilac bush. The male and female communicate to each other from here and the oak as they're building the nest. That's what all that squawking is. If you wait, you'll hear the other one answer back."

Margaret stood quietly to listen. Sure enough, the crow in the lilac bush rummaging for twigs squawked. Then, a moment later a distant squawk came from the tree. "My gosh, they're so smart."

Frank nodded. "They really are. Amazing creatures."

Margaret smiled as she looked over to see the girls going inside. "Frank, I have to check on my daughters, but we'd love to have you over next week. Dave should be home by then, and I know you two will get along great."

Frank's eyes lit up. "I'd love that."

* * *

Over at the Book Nook, a well-known professional birder was doing a presentation on birding in Cape May. Even though only twenty people signed up online for the discussion, about thirty showed up, causing Sarah to feel a little stressed about the situation.

Erin handed a customer her cappuccino, then walked over to Sarah as she stood in the back of the discussion group rubbing her temples. "You OK?"

Sarah sighed. "I mean it's great so many people came, but we were only prepared for twenty. There're only twenty chairs. Everyone else is standing. Not only that, but there isn't any room for shoppers in here."

Erin nodded in agreement. "Well, it's your first month of putting together events like this. I think you're going to learn as you go, and we're here to help with anything you need. The upside? I personally witnessed most of these people order a drink from the counter, and a bunch were perusing the book-shelves. It's definitely bringing in business."

Sarah smiled just as the birding presenter finished the hour-long talk, complete with a question-and-answer segment, and the attendees started to leave. "Mind helping me fold the chairs and bring them back in the basement?"

"Sure thing," Erin said as she looked over at Bert. He was handling the coffee counter like a pro. He glanced back at her, and they both smiled.

"So, tomorrow there's going to be a crochet class in the afternoon," Sarah said as they grabbed some chairs and headed into the basement.

Erin paused for a moment. "How many events are coming up? I thought we only had a couple reading groups on the schedule next week."

Sarah laughed nervously. "I kind of booked something every day for the next two weeks."

Just then, they heard a crash upstairs. They both ran up the steps, looking around to see where it came from until they saw it. A customer was pinned against a bookshelf after trying to maneuver behind a row of chairs towards the nonfiction book section. She had gotten her leg stuck in the rungs of the chair and had fallen.

"Are you OK?" Sarah asked as she carefully helped her up.

"I think so. Maybe just a bruise," the woman said as she brushed off her pants and stood up.

"I'm so sorry about this. We need to figure out a better plan. How about a coffee on me?" Sarah asked, feeling horrible about the situation.

The customer seemed more than happy about the offer, but Sarah now knew something needed to change if the Book Nook was going to host events more often.

* * *

"Dale, where are we going?" Donna asked as Dale drove them north on the parkway.

"It's a surprise," Dale said as he took his eyes off the road to quickly glance at Donna.

Donna gave him a look. "You're really not going to tell me?"

Dale sighed. "Fine. I'll let you know part of the surprise. We're going to Atlantic City."

"Alright …" Donna said, thoroughly confused. "Are we getting dinner?"

Dale laughed. "You're really not going to let me surprise you, are you?"

Donna shrugged. "OK, I'll stop asking questions."

An hour later, they were pulling into a casino parking garage, then walking into the casino.

"Well, this is it. We're here to see Jack Jeffries perform. I found out he had another show in Atlantic City this week," Dale said with excitement radiating from him.

"Oh, OK," Donna said, feeling a slight tinge of disappointment.

"What's the matter? You don't want to go?" Dale asked, shock all over his face.

Donna quickly changed her tune, realizing she may have hurt Dale's feelings. "Hon, I'm fine with seeing his show. I don't know, I guess I was hoping it was a dinner reservation because I'm starving." Deep down, though, she wasn't as excited about magicians as Dale.

Dale laughed. "Well, this is actually a dinner show. We'll be served dinner while we watch," he said taking her hand and leading her to the red-rope entrance.

They walked to their table—a round booth that faced the stage—and ordered some drinks and food just before the lights dimmed and the orchestra started playing music.

"Get ready for this," Dale said excitedly as he squeezed Donna's hand under the table.

Lights of different colors crossed over the stage as the music grew louder and louder, and out came Jack Jeffries with his wife and assistant, Tracy. They bowed to the audience, then immediately started the show.

Donna looked at Dale, studying how his eyes were cemented on the stage, then back at Jack Jeffries as he searched the audience for a volunteer. A gentleman was plucked from the front row and made his way on stage, coming to stand next to Jack by a large fishbowl full of water on a table.

Jack looked at the audience then back at John, his volunteer. "As you can see, this is a fishbowl full of water. Go ahead and show them by putting your hand in there."

John nodded, rolled up his sleeve, and dunked his hand in, revealing how wet it was to the audience.

Then, Jack produced some coins from his left sleeve and

handed them to John. "OK, please stick these quarters into the bowl."

John did so as the audience watched in anticipation.

Jack took a black cloth napkin from a nearby table and threw it over the top of the bowl then removed it. "Now, I want you to stick your hand into the fishbowl and pull out what's in there," Jack said as he stepped back.

John put his hand back in the bowl, and a look of confusion came over his face. He searched around in the bowl and pulled his hand out to reveal a hunk of dry sand pouring through his fingertips onto the stage. Not a drop of water was to be seen.

The audience gasped in amazement. Then, Jack walked over to the large fishbowl, picked it up and turned it upside down. Nothing came out. Not even a speck of sand from the pile John had pulled from.

The audience sat stunned in silence, waiting to see what would happen next.

Jack set the fishbowl back on the table and again placed the black cloth napkin over the fishbowl. "John, take the napkin off and reach your hand into the fishbowl once more, please."

John looked at the audience, they cheered him on, then he stuck his hand in again, this time with even more confusion on his face. He searched around for about twenty seconds, then pulled his wet hand out full of quarters.

The audience clapped and cheered as Jack thanked John before he exited the stage.

Dale looked over at Donna, who now had her eyes glued to the stage. She turned to Dale with a wide grin on her face. "OK, I'm starting to see your fascination with this now."

Dale laughed and inched closer to her, putting his arms around her shoulders just as the waitress dropped off their drinks and appetizers and the next magic trick began.

Two hours later, they were in line waiting to talk to Jack and Tracy Jeffries after the show. When it was finally their turn, Jack smiled big when he saw Dale, and gave him a handshake.

"Jack, your show was so good the first time I saw it, I had to come and see it again. This is Donna, my fiancée," Dale said proudly.

Donna held her hand out in awe, feeling like she was meeting the biggest celebrity ever. "So nice to meet you. I was absolutely wowed by your show."

Jack shook Donna's hand. "Thank you so much. That means a lot to us. By the way, this is my wife and assistant, Tracy."

Tracy smiled. "We're excited to perform at your wedding on the Fourth of July. Honestly, we've fallen in love with Cape May and are really looking forward to spending more time there."

Dale and Donna both laughed with giddiness. "We're equally excited and can't thank you two enough. We'll update you with any new details and see you then," Dale said.

Ten minutes later, they were on the parkway headed south to Cape May.

Donna couldn't stop talking about the show. "Can you believe it? How he showed up in the box Tracy was in? And how she was under the tarp that he was under? How did they pull that off?"

Dale smiled and shook his head. "We may never know. Magicians never reveal their secrets."

"How cool was it that he talked with us after the show and reminded us he'll be performing at our wedding. I guess it's really happening, huh?" Donna asked with stars in her eyes.

"I think so. He seems to be a man of his word," Dale said.

Donna sighed as she rolled down the window and let the warm summer night air whip her hair around. "I'm inspired, and I have an idea."

"What's that?" Dale asked as he turned the radio down a notch.

"I want our wedding theme to revolve around magic, especially since Jack Jeffries is putting on a show," Donna said.

"Really? Do we have time to do all of this? The wedding is next week," Dale said.

Donna tapped her fingers on the dashboard "Well, I don't think it will be that hard. It's going to take some creativity and some extra purchases, but I think we can easily pull it off and stay on budget. I have a ton of ideas running through my head right now."

CHAPTER SEVEN

Lisa pulled up a seat at the outside bar at Joe's Oyster Bar, wearing a bathing suit and shorts, with her long sun-kissed hair glowing in the hot sunlight.

"Hey, cutie," a voice said from behind the bar.

Lisa looked over the menu she was holding to see Nick had walked outside with a tray of oysters for a customer sitting across from her. "Hey, you. I just got done surfing and figured I'd stop in for some lunch."

Nick smiled from ear to ear. "Oh yeah? I feel honored," he said with a wink. "What can I start you with to drink?" he asked after handing off the oysters.

Lisa dabbed a few beads of sweat from her brow with her napkin. "How about a cold glass of ice water with lemon."

"Coming right up," Nick said as he poured the water and gave Lisa a few extra lemon slices. He handed her the drink and leaned toward her with his elbows on the bar. "Today has been something, and we've only been open a few hours," he said quietly so only she could hear.

Lisa widened her eyes in disbelief. "What happened?"

Nick looked around the bar at the other customers eating and talking, they seemed oblivious to their conversation. "Just some super nasty patrons came in. They were treating Holly, their server, horribly for no reason."

Lisa shook her head in disgust. "I'm so sorry to hear that."

Nick sighed. "They had Holly in tears. Unreal."

"What were they upset about?" Lisa asked.

"Apparently, they wanted two meals taken off the tab because they didn't like it. Funny thing is, they ate everything on their plates. Why did you eat it if you didn't like it?" Nick said quietly, clearly agitated. "Anyway, Jeremy, our manager pointed out they had already eaten all of the meals and instead generously offered them desserts on the house to keep the peace. Well, they weren't happy with that. When Jeremy walked away, they let Holly have it as they needed someone to take out their unjustified reactions on. Sweet Holly who is nothing but nice to everyone."

Lisa rubbed her hand over her face in disbelief, then reached into her purse, pulling out a twenty-dollar bill. "Give this to Holly from me. I'm sure she got stiffed. I want to help out."

Nick pushed Lisa's money back towards her. "We already all chipped in to make up for that horrendous table. Jeremy told them they weren't welcome back."

"Working in a restaurant is definitely not for the weak. I've been there," Lisa said.

Nick threw the bar towel over his shoulder and started cutting limes. "What are you ordering to eat?"

"I'm thinking the fried green tomato BLT with fries," Lisa said as she handed her menu to Nick.

"Good choice, oh, and it's on the house," he said with a wink.

Lisa shook her head. "You don't have to do that, Nick."

"Oh, I know. I want to, though," Nick said with a smile as he rang the food in on the computer, then checked on the other guests.

Lisa took out a book to read as she waited for her food.

Nick finished up with a customer and was back in front of Lisa, cleaning glasses in the sink.

Lisa set her book on the bar. "I found a place."

Nick's eyes widened as excitement took over his face. "You did? So, you're sticking around Cape May for a bit?"

Lisa smiled and nodded. "I've decided I am. It's been really great being back in Cape May. I found a month-to-month rental near Higbee Beach."

Nick cocked his head to the side. "Really? Where exactly?"

"Over by that secret beach area the locals talk about. A cute little green house with a sandy beach path," Lisa said, staring at Nick to see if it rang any bells.

"Interesting. I know where that is," Nick said as he dried the glasses with a towel.

Lisa could see the wheels turning in his head and thought about what Carrie had said. "The owner, Carrie, said she knew you. You kind of came up in conversation."

Nick set his towel down. "Yes, I know Carrie. I dated her sister, Colleen, while she lived in that house. We ended up breaking up after about six months of dating. Well, I broke up with her ..." Nick said as he stacked the glasses.

Lisa was intrigued. "Why didn't it work out?"

Nick sighed and shrugged. "She was ready for a commitment I couldn't give her."

"Interesting," Lisa said as she paused for a moment.

"What's interesting?" Nick asked curiously.

"When I brought you up to Carrie—and I said you and I were still getting to know each other ... you know, taking things slow—she was really flabbergasted by the *slow* part," Lisa said, starting to feel a little uneasy with the conversation.

"Huh," Nick said as he propped his elbows on the bar and thought for a moment. "So, she was insinuating that I don't take things slow in relationships?"

Lisa nodded. "That's how it seemed."

Nick stood up and shook his head. "I think she's going off

some one-sided information. Colleen wanted me to move in, and I wasn't ready for that. That's when we started having disagreements, and I initiated the breakup. It's really as simple as that. I haven't talked to her in years. I hear she's married now with a baby. Not sure why Carrie felt the need to talk to you about this."

Lisa sighed. "Sorry, I shouldn't have brought that up."

Nick shook his head. "Don't be sorry. I think good communication is important between two people."

Lisa dazed out in thought, her brain reciting Nick's words of "important between two people." Two people? It was so generic, not indicative of any type of relationship or romantic connection. Two people could be anybody. It could be two strangers crossing the street and one communicates to the other to watch out for a bike coming fast around the corner. Is that all they were to each other right now? Just two people? Would her asking if they were exclusive be diving in too fast? Nick was talking about the importance of communication and now Lisa felt like she was scared to communicate.

Just then, Holly brought out Lisa's BLT and fries and set it in front of her. "Enjoy," Holly said, smiling at Lisa then Nick.

"Thank you," Lisa said as she snapped out of her thoughts and looked over the beautiful plate of food. She popped a hot fry in her mouth.

Nick glanced at her plate of food. "See, I told you that was a good choice.

Lisa smiled. "It's delicious," she said, then took a bite of the BLT.

Nick tapped his fingers on the bar, then looked around to make sure nobody was listening. "I think this week is my last week working here."

"Really? Why so soon?" Lisa asked, feeling quite surprised.

"Well, working here was initially just to have money while the oyster farm built up steam, but now it's growing. We just signed on five more Philadelphia restaurants who are buying our oysters. I'm ready to invest more time in the farm and have more days off after working eighty-plus-hour weeks for the past couple of years," Nick said with a sigh of relief. "Plus, it will definitely give us more time to spend together," he said with a smile.

Lisa tried to hide the smile on her face, but it was too late.

* * *

Dave leaned on a fence post and took a deep breath at Fox Run Wildlife Refuge. The volunteers working with him also leaned on the fence, all of them catching their breath.

"Well, we did it. We built twenty new enclosures for the wildlife rescues," Dave said, feeling mighty proud of everyone.

"I can't believe it," Chuck said. "We even managed to build bottle feeders for the fawns out here."

Joyce stepped outside and walked over, stopping to look at all the hard work everyone had done. "I can't thank you all enough. You're truly making a difference. I just got word that the fires are officially out."

The group cheered, everyone dispersing except Dave and Joyce.

"Dave, you've been a blessing since you arrived. We can't thank you enough for everything you have done here," Joyce said, patting his shoulder.

Dave smiled. "I do what I can. There are even a few extra enclosures that we had time to build that you didn't ask for … just in case."

Joyce sighed with relief. "Absolutely incredible. I didn't know what we were going to do once the forest fires hit, but I'm starting to finally see the light at the end of the tunnel. Well, except we're short-staffed in the wildlife hospital. I know you're finished with the construction, but do you have any experience within the hospital? We could really use help the next couple of days. We've been low on volunteers due to people being out on vacation."

Dave paused for a moment. He hadn't expected to be asked such a thing, and a big part of him missed being at home with the girls and Margaret. Actually, Margaret especially, as they'd barely had much time to talk with how busy Dave had been. "I do have experience in the hospital. I'm fine with staying a few extra days if you need help."

Joyce smiled. "Thank you, Dave. You're amazing."

"No problem. I'm going to go get dinner. I'll see you in the hospital tomorrow," Dave said as he headed to his truck.

Fifteen minutes later, he pulled into a parking lot and walked into a diner. "Table for one," he said to the host before being led to a booth by the window.

Dave ordered a soda and the chicken pot pie, then called Margaret.

"Hey, you. How's it going up there?" Margaret asked.

Dave smiled at the sound of Margaret's voice. "It's going great. We finished all twenty of the new enclosures today."

Margaret's eyes widened. "You didn't tell me you were building twenty. My gosh, that's a lot."

Dave laughed. "Well, the volunteers were workhorses. A great group of people, and Fox Run Wildlife Refuge is a lot more spread out than Pinetree. There's plenty of room for the new enclosures. The animals will be safe and sound while they await their release back into nature. Anyway, how are things at home? I'm quite homesick."

"Things are great. I've just been tidying up the garden. The girls have been enjoying the yard, swinging on the tire swing you put up, and running through the sprinklers. Oh … I met Frank next door," Margaret said as she slumped into a chair and twirled her hair.

"Frank?" Dave asked confused.

"Our neighbor next door. His name is Frank. He's wonderful. He's widowed and lives alone. He misses his wife dearly, the poor soul. Anyway, we're going to have him over when you get home. He knows a lot about our land and gardening, and well, he's just a really neat person."

Dave smiled. "Wow. He sounds great. I can't wait to meet him when I get home. About that, they asked me to stay a few extra days to help with the influx of animals in the hospital since I have experience. I really didn't want to stay, but …"

"You should stay. They need you. I know the feeling of being bombarded in the wildlife hospital. It's stressful," Margaret said.

"Well, I agreed to stay. I couldn't tell them no, but I miss you," Dave said as his iced tea arrived.

Margaret felt her heart turn to mush as she looked out the window at some geese flying by. "Dave, I miss you like crazy. We've never been apart this long before, have we?"

Dave took a sip of his drink and laughed. "No, never. Now I know why."

Margaret suddenly felt like a high schooler talking to her long-distance summer romance. She watched as the girls walked up to her and stood there.

"Is that Dave?" Harper asked.

Margaret nodded. "Yes, want to talk to him?"

Harper and Abby both nodded, and Margaret put the phone on speaker.

"Hi, girls," Dave said cheerfully.

"Dave, when are you going to be home?" Abby asked.

"Probably in four days."

"Good. It's too lonely and quiet in the house," Harper said as she turned around and trekked upstairs. Abby followed her.

Margaret dropped her mouth open. "Lonely? Am I chopped liver?" she called up the stairs.

Dave laughed. "Did they leave?"

Margaret rolled her eyes. "Yes. They insulted me, then left. Apparently, I'm not enough for them," she said with a chuckle.

"Well, you're enough for me," Dave said as his chicken pot pie arrived.

Margaret blushed and threw her head back. "I'm going to attempt to clean up the yard and mow the grass for the wedding before you arrive. You've been working so hard. It'll be one less thing for you to worry about."

Dave shook his head. "Honestly, leave it. I'll do it when I get back. I enjoy doing it."

"Look, I'm a girl who gets her hands dirty. I'm a true gardener and yard-work lover. I think I can handle it," Margaret said as she walked into the kitchen.

Dave sighed. "Fine. I'm not going to stop you. You're a go-getter, that's for sure. It's partly why I fell for you."

"Oh yeah? When did you fall for me?" Margaret asked.

Dave took a bite of his dinner and swallowed. "I probably shouldn't say."

"Why?" Margaret asked.

"Because it was back when I never said a word to you at Pinetree Refuge," Dave said. "I was too scared to talk to you, plus you were married. I didn't want to mess with that."

Margaret was taken aback. "So, it was before we became friends and started hanging out?"

Dave laughed. "Yes, wasn't it obvious? The way I would ignore you whenever I came into the hospital to get something?"

"Oh, totally obvious. Nothing like a guy ignoring your exis-tence to truly show you how much they like you," Margaret said sarcastically.

"Well, I had a little crush. That's for sure. You were unde-niably beautiful, and still are. You were so nice to the staff, and I loved hearing your laugh from the hospital when I was outside working. It always made me happy," Dave said as he stared off into the distance, remembering it all.

"David Patterson, how come you never told me this?" Margaret asked, feeling herself blush even more.

Dave shrugged. "I don't know. I didn't want to sound like a creep when I met you, and then I just forgot about it."

"Well, I'm glad you told me. I thought you were pretty cute yourself … even if you did ignore me," Margaret said as she opened the refrigerator, looking for something to cook the girls for dinner.

Dave laughed. "I can't wait to see you."

CHAPTER EIGHT

It was another hot summer day in Cape May Point, and Judy was working her second shift as a beach tag checker. She schlepped her clunky chair and large umbrella up the sandy beach path until she found her spot right at the bottom of the entrance.

With sweat pouring from her face, she kneeled down to twist the umbrella's anchor into the ground. The seagulls hovered overhead, seemingly eyeing up her bag to see if any food was in there, while two people played paddle ball twenty feet away, hitting a ball back and forth as the ocean waves peacefully crashed in the distance. The sand was treacherously hot, and Judy could feel it starting to burn her feet through her sandals.

Popping the umbrella into the anchor, Judy opened it up, then sat down in her chair with the biggest sigh of relief. She fanned herself with her paperback book and took a long sip of water from her water bottle. Then, she checked that she had dollar bills for change in her fanny pack and powered on the credit card reader. When she was finally settled, she turned around to get a good look at the ocean, but it was behind her and hard to see over everyone on the beach.

The first couple to walk on the beach looked at Judy as they walked by but didn't stop.

"Oh, hi. Do you have your beach tags?" Judy asked.

The guy looked annoyed. "We have to pay to get on the beach now?"

Judy was taken aback. It was common knowledge that Coral Avenue beach required tags, but maybe it was their first time there. "Yes, the fees go towards paying our lifeguards and keeping our beaches clean, among other things."

"Hon, just pay her for two beach tags," his wife said, looking rather embarrassed. "We're used to going to the beaches in Strathmere where it's free," she said to Judy.

Judy smiled and nodded as they handed her cash, and she gave them two beach tags.

Two hours had gone by, and by then many beachgoers had come onto the beach, but it had started to slow down, and Judy finally had a minute to open her book. She had just bought a new paperback over at the Book Nook and was excited to dive in. It was a thriller that a friend had recommended.

Just as she was two pages in, the wind picked up on the beach, sending her umbrella high in the sky before it inverted and crashed back down onto the sand.

Judy jumped out of her seat, noticing she hadn't tightened the screw into the umbrella pole. She ran over to her umbrella and picked it up only to find it was completely broken, as it wouldn't even open anymore.

"Guess I won't be using an umbrella. I only have a couple more hours. I should be able to make it," Judy said to herself.

However, within ten minutes, her feet were on fire, and she felt her shoulders burning even though she had put on sunblock. Sweat poured from her, and she wasn't sure how much longer she was going to last.

Minutes later, she decided she couldn't take it any anymore, so she called Bob.

"Hi, dear," Bob answered joyfully.

"Bob, are you at home?" Judy asked, more uncomfortable by the minute.

"I am, but I'm about to leave to go volunteer at Animal Outreach. What's up?"

Judy looked around the beach. "I'm stuck on the beach for the next hour and a half with a broken umbrella. I feel sick to my stomach. I don't think I can handle this heat without some type of shade. Can you grab the extra umbrella in the garage and drive it over to me?"

Bob nodded. "I know exactly where it is. I'll be there in ten minutes."

Ten long minutes later, Judy saw Bob walking up the beach path holding the umbrella. She felt like someone stranded on a desert island by that point and seeing Bob was the best thing she'd seen in a while. She rubbed her eyes to make sure she wasn't dreaming.

"Here, let me set it up for you," Bob said as he approached and kneeled down in the sand to get the umbrella anchored and opened.

"You literally saved the day, Bob. I was starting to think that an ambulance was going to have to be called if I didn't get out of this heat," Judy said as she hugged him.

* * *

Bob headed to Animal Outreach of Cape May County for his first volunteer shift. After pulling into a parking spot, he arrived inside to the cheerful staff and volunteers. It was mostly volunteer run, aside from a couple staff members, and a lot of the folks had been there for at least a couple years.

The facility was located in a converted dentist office with different rooms for the free-roaming cats so they weren't cooped up in cages all day. They also adopted out dogs, but they were kept in foster homes.

Bob was impressed with the facility and how well run it

was. "Here, let me give you a tour before you start," a volunteer said. "I'm Trish. I've been volunteering here for years. It's so rewarding. You're going to love it."

After the tour, Bob was assigned one of the cat rooms to clean. There, he washed the food dishes and water bowls, then swept the floor.

Trish popped her head into the room. "How are you making out, Bob?"

Bob smiled. "It's going good. I think I'm just about done cleaning this room."

Trish nodded. "That's great. You're a cat person, I'm assuming?"

Bob laughed. "Well, not exactly. We have a dog at home, one we rescued off the beach in Ocean City, Maryland. I've always been a dog person."

Trish sighed. "That's how I started out. Had dogs all my life. Never really liked cats, but then my husband talked me into adopting a cat from here, and I can't imagine life without Daisy. Now I'm here volunteering. It's funny how these little animals can change your life for the better," Trish said as she picked up a cat toy and left.

Bob looked around the room, feeling happy with his cleaning skills. Judy would be proud, that's for sure. He sat down in a nearby chair as the cats napped quietly in different beds and hammocks. Suddenly, he felt a tap on his leg and heard a quiet *meow* come from below. He looked down to see a chunky orange tabby named Bruce trying to get his attention.

"Well, hello there, fella," Bob said as he reached down to pet Bruce's head. Bruce happily chirped and extended his neck so Bob could reach better.

Within moments, Bruce had decided he needed to be more up close and personal, so he jumped onto Bob's lap, purring furiously as he found the perfect spot to curl up.

Bob pet Bruce while he kept happily chirping and purring.

"I see we both like a good comfortable seat," Bob said with a chuckle.

Trish poked her head back into the room. "Well, I'll be. Looks like Bruce really likes you."

Bob nodded as he continued petting him. "He's a friendly guy, that's for sure."

Trish nodded. "I'm surprised Bruce hasn't been adopted yet. One of the friendliest cats in the building. We're even told he likes dogs. Apparently, his best friend was a dog at his old home."

"You're kidding," Bob said, surprised. I wonder how Hugo would feel about a cat, he thought to himself.

* * *

That afternoon, Chris and Eric had hosed off the decks of the birding boats, getting them ready for the next cruise set to board in ten minutes.

The dock was packed with people who had signed up for the birding cruises—enough to completely fill both boats to the max.

"It's a good thing I got the second boat. Look at all these people," Chris said as he put his hand on Eric's shoulder. "Do you think you're set for your first day here as a captain?"

Eric waved his hand in the air. "Oh, for sure. I'm more than ready."

"Perfect. Just follow my lead, and I'm sure everything will go fine," Chris said as he walked over towards his new boat and attached the ramp to the dock. He waved to everyone on the dock. "OK, you can all board now. We're going to fill up my boat first, then Eric's. Make sure you stay with your party."

Five minutes later, Chris's boat was full, and leaving the dock. "Eric, you good? You know where I'm heading first, right?" Chris yelled over to Eric.

Eric gave Chris a thumbs-up. "I've got it. Go on ahead."

Chris made his way out onto the bay, passing different marshlands while scoping for the best spot to stop and watch shorebirds. "Ah, perfect. We've got a ton of egrets over here," he said pointing. The birders on the boat all immediately moved to the other side to view the white birds with binoculars.

Chris looked out over the water, trying to find Eric and his second boat. It'd been fifteen minutes, so he should have been close by already. He dialed Eric on his cell phone, but it went straight to voicemail.

Twenty minutes later, Chris had moved the boat to the second location, another marshlands spot, but this time there were blue herons looking for fish to eat. While everyone on the boat watched the birds search for food, Chris still couldn't find Eric. He called again, and it went to voicemail once more.

"Must have forgotten to charge his phone or something," Chris said out loud as he put his phone in his pocket.

About an hour later, it was time to head back. It was a nice half hour boat ride back to the dock. By this point, Chris could only hope that Eric had figured out where to go for his birding cruise, as he was still missing in action.

Then, there it was. Eric and the boat he captained appeared alongside Chris's.

"Hey, Chris!" Eric yelled over loud dance music playing on board his boat.

Chris shifted his eyes. He yelled back, but they were too far apart, and the wind and loud music made it hard to hear anything.

Chris glanced over at Eric's boat to see people dancing out on the deck and inside, all of them holding plastic cups full of liquid. It looked like a party boat. His stomach immediately dropped.

"What is happening over there?" he said out loud, frustrated as he steered.

When they got back to the dock, after the birders all left the boats, Chris needed answers.

"Eric, what was going on on your boat? Loud music, dancing, beverages? Please tell me that wasn't alcohol," Chris said.

Eric rubbed his temples. "I'm so sorry. Someone brought a cooler on board. I figured it was just water or sodas, but it was alcohol. They had already poured it into cups and passed it out before I realized the whole boat had drinks. The same person brought a portable speaker and started playing music."

Chris shook his head. "Look. There are party boats with bars on board in Cape May that people can do that stuff on. I'm all about having a good time, but we offer a different experience here on the Blue Heron Birding Boats, one that is more educational and peaceful. I like to focus on the tranquility of nature. Not to mention, we're birding. Loud music is just going to chase away all the wildlife. It's simply not what my business is about. You have to tell people no next time that happens. By the way, where did you go? You never made it to any of the locations I told you I'd be at."

Eric shrugged. "I made a wrong turn, and when I realized it and made my way to the second location, you were already gone. By that point, I just followed my own route."

"Did you see any birds?" Chris asked, bewildered.

Eric nodded. "Actually, yes. We saw a ton. Egrets, herons, skimmers, osprey, you name it."

"Skimmers? You serious? Where? I've been having a hard time finding them lately," Chris asked with complete curiosity.

"On that first turn, there's a small little section of marshlands that juts out. Can't miss 'em," Eric said, pointing off towards the water.

"Seriously? I hadn't seen anything back there in a while. I've been bypassing that area for months now. I guess I shouldn't anymore," Chris said as he rubbed his chin in thought.

"I definitely wouldn't skip it anymore. There were also quite a few oyster catchers back there too," Eric said.

"You know your stuff. It's why I hired you, but do me a favor? Can you keep your phone charged and on? I called you multiple times and couldn't reach you. It went straight to voicemail."

Eric stared off into the distance, realizing he had made a pretty big mistake. "I screwed up today. I'm so sorry. My phone died right before we left the dock, and I forgot to mention that to you. Also, I should have said something to those people passing alcohol out and playing music. I don't know why I didn't."

"It's OK. You didn't know how you should've handled the situation, but hopefully you do now?" Chris asked.

Eric nodded. "Definitely. I'll go over the rules after everyone boards before we leave the dock next time."

Chris chuckled. "It figures that you get that group of people on your first day here. All these years, I've never dealt with that myself. Well, you definitely had a good learning experience today. We'll knock the sunset tour out of the park this evening."

"So, I'm not fired?" Eric asked.

"No, of course not. When I was your age, I made mistakes on boats. You're not alone," Chris laughed.

"Oh yeah?" Eric said, a smile forming on his face.

Chris took a deep breath. "Yeah, and my dad will never let me live it down. We were out in the ocean on a fishing trip on my uncle's boat for the day. There were about six of us. My dad was helping bait the hooks on the rods, and a wave came, rocking the boat side to side. I slipped and fell back, knocking all the rods straight into the ocean. Needless to say, that fishing trip was cut quite short."

Eric laughed. "You're kidding? How does that even happen?"

Chris chuckled as he remembered the entire scenario. "It

was something out of a cartoon. I just remember seeing the shocked look on my dad's face as the rods fell forward and off the boat in slow motion. My uncles all dove to try and save them as I watched, frozen in horrified shock. They won't let me live it down. Every family gathering, it's brought up. Luckily, we all laugh about it now."

Eric nudged Chris. "Well, you live and you learn."

CHAPTER NINE

Decked out in overalls and a mask, Liz ran the electric sander back and forth over the dresser she had thrifted earlier in the week. After a few minutes, she took off her mask and grabbed her water bottle, gulping the cold water furiously.

"How's it going in here?" Greg asked as he walked into the garage from outside. Liz had the doors propped open for fresh air.

"It's going," she said in between gulps of water. "It's just so hot in here. I've got the doors open, but there's isn't a breeze since there's nothing to open up in the back of the garage," Liz said pointing.

"Nonsense. We can probably prop open that little window back there," Greg said as he walked over to inspect it.

Liz shook her head. "It's been nailed shut since we bought the property. Probably painted shut too. If you want to give it a try, go ahead. It just seems like it's too much work right now."

Greg thought for a moment. "How about I bring some fans out for you?"

"Then I'll have sanding dust everywhere. It's actually already everywhere," she said looking around.

"Well, the dresser is looking great," Greg said as he ran his hand across it. "Wasn't this full of scratches and water stains?"

Liz nodded. "Yes, and dirt and dust. I gave it a good cleaning first, then went to work sanding it. Now, I have to stain it and polish up the hardware. It's going to look amazing afterwards. It will be totally restored and look almost brand-new once I'm done with it. I've already finished the end tables. Come take a look," Liz said as she brought him towards a tarp.

Liz lifted the tarp off to reveal the completely refurbished end tables sitting happily under it. "You wouldn't believe the amount of crud I got off these. I think they must have been in someone's kid's room, because there was a lot of chewed gum stuck underneath them that I had to scrape off."

Greg shook his head in amazement. "They're gorgeous. Absolutely stunning."

"Thank you," Liz said as she picked up a brush and a can of wood stain and headed back to the dresser where she started painting it on the drawers. "It's really felt great to get back into this. I think I forgot how much I loved to get my hands dirty on my own time."

"Well, what's the plan? What are you going to do with this set after you're finished?" Greg asked as he watched Liz meticulously paint the stain on.

"Well, I'm going to list pieces for sale on social media and see what happens from there. If there's a lot of interest, I'll continue to refurbish and sell furniture, and if there isn't, I may just make this a hobby," Liz said.

"This is quite exciting. I'm glad to see you using your time doing something you love. I know losing that client was rough for you," Greg said as his eyes softened.

Liz stopped painting and stood up, turning to the left and right to stretch her back. "It was rough, but I'm not letting it bring me down. I think I'll have this dresser finished tonight. Then tomorrow morning, with the sunlight, I'll get some great photos before putting the set for sale. I'm excited."

Lisa stood outside her new cute beach house rental holding the key in one hand and her suitcase in the other. "Well, this is it. I guess I'm really staying in Cape May for a bit," she said out loud as she approached the front door.

She turned the key in the lock, and instantly felt a sense of relief. She'd been on the road in her van for months since leaving Hawaii, and now she finally had a place to call her own. In fact, it was her first place alone. She had lived with her husband in Hawaii, and when she found out he was not only cheating but had a whole other family, it was time for a divorce and to leave the island.

Before she could shut the door, she heard a familiar voice.

"Hey, you," Nick said as he leaned on the door frame. "I came here to help you move in, but I didn't see anything else in the van to bring in when I checked."

Lisa laughed. "All I've got is this suitcase and my laptop. I've been living the simple life on the road, which is why this furnished house is perfect for me," she said as she sat down on the couch and kicked her feet up on the ottoman.

Nick did the same. "I have to say, it does look different in here since I last saw it. They painted and redid the kitchen. It looks great. Do you need to unpack? Can I help with anything?"

Lisa looked around the living room, then shook her head. "No, I can do that later. Let's go explore. I don't know this little section of Cape May very well."

Nick's eyes lit up. "I know the area. I'll show you the spots," he said, hopping off the couch to lead the way out of the house and towards the sandy beach path out to the road.

Lisa followed him through another sandy trail full of tall pine trees until they got to a wooden platform bordered by overgrown vegetation near the dunes.

"This may seem like something you see on a lot of beach

paths in Cape May," Nick said as he sat down on a bench, "but we did some night fishing out here, and this is the perfect spot to see the stars on a clear night. I think it's because it's a more secluded beach, so you don't have all that light pollution over here. Of course, you can opt to walk the beach or even sit on it, but I actually built this platform with my brothers and my dad years ago. It's since been redone to replace the rotting wood, but it's still our original work."

Lisa leaned on the railing. "You're kidding. That's really special, and it's high enough to see way down the beach on both sides. It's the perfect spot for a morning coffee or an evening glass of wine."

Nick turned to look at the bench, then ran his hands over a small gold metal plate. "We didn't build this bench, but we did make a donation to dedicate it in honor of my grandmother. That's her name there, Barbie."

Lisa walked over to the bench and ran her fingers over the plate, feeling the smoothness of it. "I see how this all means so much to you. How often do you come over here?"

Nick shrugged. "Honestly, I haven't been here in a long time. Maybe since I dated Colleen …"

Lisa paused in thought then blurted it out. "I know we talked a little about this, but have you been in any serious relationships recently? What's your dating life like? Carrie threw me a curve ball when she started talking about your past relationship, because I didn't know anything about it. Should we talk about this stuff?"

Nick sat for a moment and thought. "I was in a serious relationship for about five years once. Her name was Tammy. Honestly, I think it just hit us both one day that we weren't right for each other. I went to her to discuss breaking up, and she'd been thinking about when to bring it up to me. Since then, it's been friends trying to set me up with their friends, and nothing really clicked, including with Colleen. I've been quite alone for a number of years, living the bachelor life. I decided to focus on my career and myself, and it's really been incredible. Then you came around, and suddenly I feel happier than I have in a while."

Lisa blushed, unsure what to say. Nick was so genuine, but she was really starting to wonder where they stood. Maybe he was happy living alone while casually dating someone. Was that what she wanted, though?

Before Lisa could saying anything, Nick took her hand. "I've got one more thing to show you. Follow me," he said leading her towards the beach. He searched the sky, then pointed. "There's the Cape May Lighthouse."

The waves lapped gently as Lisa stared at the distant light coming from the lighthouse. "Oh, I love that. I didn't think we'd see it from here," she said as she looked up at all the stars shining in the sky.

Nick pulled her in close for a kiss just as the moon appeared from behind a cloud.

* * *

Margaret was finished with work and was now outside getting the yard ready for the wedding with her earbuds in listening to music. She found an electric trimmer in the shed that had been left behind with the house, plugged it in, and got to work on the overgrown boxwoods.

As she was finishing trimming the third boxwood, the power cut out on the trimmer.

"Oh no. Did I yank the plug out by accident?" Margaret said out loud as she walked to the side of the house where the outlet was. "Nope. It's still plugged in," she said, not sure of what happened.

Margaret walked over and picked up the trimmer, this time studying it up and down. Then, she smacked it a couple times and it miraculously came back on. She shrugged and went back to trimming the bushes again, but minutes later, it turned off once more.

"This is annoying. I'm assuming it's not the breaker box since it did come back on. It just must be old and shot," Margaret said as she tossed it off to the side. She eyed the yard, trying to figure out what she could tackle next to lessen Dave's load when he got home. That's when her bright idea came. She'd mow the grass.

Since their property was so large, they used a tractor for most of it, and a riding mower for some smaller areas closer to the house. Margaret opened the big barn doors, revealing a red tractor. It was a bit intimidating as it was hard to get into. She had to heave herself up and then climb into the seat. Once up there, it felt like she was twenty feet in the air. As she started backing the tractor out of the barn, she let off the gas and paused for a moment. Should I be attempting this? I've only driven this once, she thought to herself.

Margaret shook the thoughts out of her head and pressed the gas pedal, backing the tractor all the way out of the barn, but as she shifted out of reverse and into drive, the tractor made a horrible sound and stalled. "Not again!" Margaret yelled out.

Margaret attempted again to go forward with the tractor, but it wouldn't budge, and instead a plume of smoke came out. "I'm done. If I do anymore, I'm going to break this tractor," she said, jumping out of it.

Just then, a loud crash came from the front of the house, causing Margaret to nearly jump out of her skin. She ripped her earbuds out and ran towards the porch to see a large tree limb had fallen onto the driveway, completely blocking it.

"What in the world?!" Margaret screamed out as she approached the limb. She looked up at the tree it had fallen from, trying to figure out what caused it. There wasn't a clear answer, so she attempted to move it off the driveway.

"This thing is heavy. How scary if someone would have

been standing or even driving here," she said as she managed to budge it three feet with a ton of effort. Margaret eventually got the entire branch pushed off to the side of the driveway, and at this point, she'd had it with yard work.

"I really hope we can get the property in shape before the wedding. This is proving to be a lot more difficult on my own than I thought it'd be," Margaret murmured to herself.

She didn't dare tell Dave yet. He already felt guilty about not being there. She didn't need to stress him out, especially when he was doing such commendable work at Fox Run Wildlife Refuge.

* * *

Donna was at home working on the new magic theme for the wedding. She'd bought different crafting materials online and was trying to decorate glass mason jars with ribbon and a glue gun when the power went out.

She walked outside to see the electric company working on the wires down the street. "How long will the power be out for?" Donna yelled towards the workers.

One of the guys shrugged. "Sorry about that. There's been an issue on this block for weeks we're told. Have you noticed lights flickering in your house?"

Donna widened her eyes. "Yes, actually. It was just two lamps, though. I thought maybe the bulbs were not screwed in tight enough."

The worker nodded. "Well, we're getting it fixed. We won't be too much longer."

Donna thanked them, then looked at her watch. Dale was working still. Maybe she'd take her supplies to Donna's Restaurant where she could have dinner and work on finishing up her project …

Fifteen minutes later, she walked inside the restaurant carrying a large cardboard box full of supplies. She set the box down on a table in the back of the restaurant as Dale approached.

"You've come to hang out with us?" Dale teased Donna.

Donna sighed as she sat down. "The power went out, and I had to get out of the house. It's lonely there, and I'm hungry and trying to finish decorating these jars for the wedding. Is this back table free?"

Dale nodded. "Of course. What can I get you from the kitchen?"

Donna smiled. "Cobb salad and an unsweetened iced tea, please."

"Coming right up," Dale said as he leaned over to hug and kiss her, then scurried off towards the kitchen.

The restaurant wasn't crazy busy yet, but business usually picked up in an hour or so. There were a few couples sitting at the bar, and maybe five tables in the dining area that had ordered food.

Dixie walked up behind Donna and put her hand on her shoulder. "Well, what have we got here?"

Donna looked up at her. "Glue guns, ribbons, and jars. For the wedding, of course. Want to help?" she asked jokingly.

"Actually, I do. I'm finished and waiting for my husband to pick me up, and he likes to take his good ol' time," she said as she pulled up a seat to the table and took a jar out of the box.

Donna smiled and held up a finished mason jar. "This is how it's supposed to look. I'm gluing the ribbon on. Pretty easy."

Dixie nodded. "I can do that easy peasy."

Ten minutes later, half of the restaurant staff was sitting at the table helping Donna, and by the time Dale brought her Cobb salad out, the jars were finished.

CHAPTER TEN

It was the perfect sunny morning, and Judy managed to get on the beach early for her shift. She positioned her umbrella and chair so she could greet the people coming up the path but also see the ocean.

After checking the beach tags of a few families that were out nice and early, she settled into her chair, sinking her feet into the shaded, cool sand. She looked out towards the ocean and breathed in the salt air. It made her feel so refreshed. Out in the ocean she watched as a sailboat glided by and then the dolphin pod appeared. This time, she didn't have to stand up to see the dolphins, as she had the perfect viewing spot, and it made her feel full of glee.

More and more people were coming onto the beach as the day went on, and for once, nothing was going wrong. Her umbrella was locked in, her sunblock and sunhat were on, and the credit card reader hadn't had one issue yet. It was a Fourth-of-July-week miracle.

Suddenly, a familiar face appeared on the beach path in the distance. Judy squinted her eyes to get a better look. She smiled when the face came into view.

"Hi, dear," Bob said as he set up his chair next to Judy under the umbrella.

Judy gave him a hug. "What a nice surprise. You decided you needed a day in the sun?"

Bob chuckled. "Not exactly. I just wanted to bring you breakfast and check on you. I know you had a rough couple of days doing this," he said, reaching into his cooler.

He pulled out two breakfast burritos, and Judy's eyes widened. "You went to Westside Market? Oh, you're spoiling me," she said while unwrapping her burrito.

Bob started to eat his breakfast but stopped when he heard the seagulls circling above.

"It's fine. Just stay under the umbrella so they don't see you," Judy said as she took a bite of her burrito.

Bob took a bite and rolled his eyes back in his head. "Nothing like a meal on the beach."

Judy nodded. "Are you volunteering today?"

"Not today, but I'll go back soon. By the way, there's a cat I want you to meet. His name is Bruce." Bob said as he took another bite.

Judy smiled. "Oh yeah? Is he your favorite over there?"

"You could say that. We've formed a bond. He loves to sit on laps, and he'll tap you with his paw for pets. He's very sociable and loving. I think you'd love him," Bob said as his eyes softened.

"He's up for adoption?" Judy asked.

Bob nodded. "I don't think he has any applications in on him, and I hear he gets along with dogs."

Judy chuckled. "So, you want me to meet him so we can adopt him. Are you nervous about how Hugo will act, though?"

Bob shook his head. "I've thought about it, but I see how Hugo acts with some of the indoor/outdoor cats near our house on walks. He pays them no mind."

"Tomorrow I'll go and meet him," Judy said as she nudged

Bob playfully, noticing they were both done eating. "Where are you headed after here?"

"I'm staying with you today. Keeping you company," he said as he whipped out a crossword puzzle book. "I'm prepared too." Bob searched for a pen unsuccessfully.

Judy laughed. "Lucky you, I have a pen in my bag, and lucky me, I get to have company on the job. Wait until you see the dolphins. They're quite the spectacle."

* * *

Across town at the Book Nook, Sarah and Erin strained to get the back door to open.

"What is behind this door anyway?" Erin asked as she twisted and pulled the doorknob with all her might.

"I just talked with the former owner, and apparently there's a little outdoor yard area. They covered it with weed barrier and stones but never used it and forgot to tell me about it since they never went out there," Sarah said as she took a turn trying to open it.

"So, where did you think this door went to, exactly?" Erin asked.

Sarah shrugged. "Honestly, I had no idea. I didn't pay it any mind since my business was inside, but now …"

The door finally flung open, taking part of the paint on the door frame with it. Fresh air immediately billowed inside, and Erin and Sarah stood with their mouths dropped open. Before them was a yard the length of the building surrounded by a six-foot wooden fence and filled with stones just like the owners had said—except some weeds had gone through the weed barrier and were now six feet high.

Erin stepped outside in shock. "It's so shady out here with the trees on either side. It's wonderful. Imagine all you could do with this space. How did we not know about this?"

Sarah chuckled. "I don't know, but I think we've found our

solution for all the events taking over the floor space—at least when it's nice weather."

"You're onto something here," Erin said, nodding.

Sarah crossed her arms and studied the yard. "I've got an idea. We're going to let Bert take care of the customers inside, and you and I are going to buy a few supplies to fix this up out here."

"I'm game. I love a good transformation," Erin said as she headed back indoors behind Sarah.

Three hours later, they had pulled all the weeds, added colorful cascading flowers in pots, and set up some folding tables and chairs.

Sarah hung the last string of white lights in the yard with a zip tie to the tree branch, then glanced at Erin and sighed. "I think this about does it. We're ready to host events out here."

Erin nodded. "It's a crime that we've never used this space before. It's wonderful. In fact, I think it's the perfect courtyard for guests to enjoy drinks while they read."

Sarah smacked her head. "Why didn't I think that of that? I was only thinking about having the events out here, but you're right. I need to get some café type tables and chairs out here. We'll just close it off when there are events but keep it open otherwise."

"Whoa!" Bert said as he peeked outside. "What is all of *this*?"

Sarah laughed. "A new extension to the Book Nook. We're going to put the events out here, and once I get some tables and chairs, customers will be allowed out here to drink, eat, and read."

Erin clapped her hands together. "OK, I have some ideas. How about some outdoor couches in that corner and that corner," she said pointing. "Maybe a couple fire pits for the fall months? Then! I think we could power wash this fence and maybe get an Airstream where we could serve drinks from along the fence there. Just *think* of all the possibilities."

"Whoa. Whoa. Whoa," Sarah said while chuckling. "This is sounding way out of my budget. It might take some time to work up to all of that, but I'm liking some of those ideas of yours."

Erin laughed. "Sorry, I get too excited about this kind of stuff. Either way, I'm optimistic about this new space."

Sarah nodded and smiled. "Me too. Me too."

* * *

That evening, Donna, Sarah, Margaret, Liz, and Lisa were in bathing suits on paddleboards right off Chris's dock, and it was a sight to be seen.

Donna paddled slowly on the bay as she tried to maintain her balance while standing. "Look, guys. I'm doing it!"

Sarah was still sitting on her knees on her board, terrified to stand up like everyone else. "I'm not sure this is for me. I might have to just stay like this the whole time," she said half-jokingly.

Clara, the yoga instructor was ahead, leading the way by paddling to a quiet and serene area of the bay, away from boats. "Everyone, we're almost there. It gets easier, trust me."

Margaret and Liz paddled along as they watched in amazement as Lisa paddled by everyone like a professional.

"Look at you!" Margaret yelled to Lisa.

Lisa laughed. "It's all that surfing experience."

They finally got to a small quiet alcove by some wetlands that was all to themselves, away from any boats.

Clara stood on her board and smiled at everyone as they paddled up beside her. "Welcome everyone to my first full moon paddleboard yoga lesson. I hope you're ready to get quite a workout in while enjoying the serene nature around us."

Liz smiled. "We're ready. This is actually somewhat of an

impromptu bachelorette party for Donna over there. She's getting married on the Fourth of July."

"How exciting. Congratulations," Clara said as everyone clapped and cheered. "Now, one important thing to note about yoga on a paddleboard is you want to keep a wide stance when standing up so you can stay stable on your board. However, we will be doing sitting poses as well."

One hour and a lot of sweat and sore muscles later, the ladies felt amazing as they dried off while walking back to the parking lot.

"So, the party continues back at my place," Margaret said as she hopped into her car. "I hope you all packed bags."

Donna laughed. "I certainly did. By the way, has anyone heard from the guys? I wonder how the Phillies game is going."

Liz looked at her phone. "Greg just sent a photo of all of them in their stadium seats."

Margaret peeked at the photo on Liz's phone. "Dave made it. I'm so glad he did."

Sarah craned her neck to see the photo as well. "Was Dave not supposed to be home yet?"

Margaret shook her head. "He was supposed to come home tomorrow morning, but when he heard about the impromptu bachelor party at the baseball game, he worked late yesterday to get everything caught up in the wildlife hospital. He's quite a professional with feeding those baby animals," Margaret said as her heart swooned. "He's staying overnight at Greg's so that us girls have the house to ourselves tonight. My parents have the kids for the evening."

Donna smiled as she looked at the photo along with everyone else. "I can tell Dale is having the time of his life. Look at the big smile," she said as she plopped into her car. "OK, see you all over at Margaret's."

Twenty minutes later, they were back at Margaret and Dave's. Margaret put on some music and ran around putting out cheese plates, multiple dips with chips, and popping the hot dogs in blankets into the oven. Meanwhile, Liz called in for a pizza delivery.

After plenty of drinks, food, and discussion, they set up five twin air mattresses in the living room, complete with sheets and comforters from Margaret's upstairs closet, though everyone had brought their own pillow.

They each got into their pajamas and sat on their respective mattresses, all staring at one another and laughing.

"We're really doing this, an adult sleepover. My gosh, I haven't had a sleepover since I was a teenager," Donna said with a bright blue clay face mask on and holding a glass of wine.

Sarah laughed, and tapped the pink fluffy slippers she was wearing together. "So, what do we do? Keep it nostalgic? How about we talk about boys like the good ol' days."

Everyone in the room laughed.

Liz adjusted her red flannel pajamas and pointed to the TV. "We could do that or put on a romantic comedy."

"How about both," Lisa said as she crossed her legs and propped her pillow up against the wall.

Donna laughed and stared at Lisa. "Well, then, you go first."

Lisa blushed. "Well, Nick and I are good. I still don't know if we're official, but we're chugging along."

Liz bit her lip. "Do you want to be official? I thought you weren't ready to set down roots in Cape May yet."

Lisa nodded. "You're right. I'm not ready, which is why I have the month-to-month rental instead of a yearlong lease, but between us … I probably will be ready if Nick shows me he wants to be in a serious relationship."

Margaret cleared her throat. "Well, it sounds like you guys are heading in that direction."

Lisa sighed. "We will see. I'm going to enjoy the ride and look out for myself in the process. I don't need any more hurt after that awful divorce."

Donna nodded. "Divorces are rough, but you made it out alive and better than ever. I'm so glad you're back in Cape May."

Lisa grabbed Donna's hand and took a sip of her wine. "I'm so glad to be here, and I'm so happy for you and Dale. You two are meant for each other."

Everyone else nodded in agreement.

"You two really are. We can see how much you love Dale and how much he loves you, and I can't wait for the wedding," Sarah said, getting choked up.

Donna smiled and looked over at Margaret. "How's Dave doing?"

Margaret sat up on her mattress. "He's great, but we really miss each other. It's a little hard knowing he'll be in Cape May tonight, and I have to wait to see him until tomorrow morning."

"Aw," Liz said as she held her heart. "Maybe you can sneak in a meetup for a hug and kiss later."

Margaret waved her hand in the air. "No, it's fine. I think it's healthy for us to finally miss each other for once. I can wait until the morning."

Sarah chimed in. "Well, Chris and I are doing well. We've both been busy with our businesses, but we've started making plans to take some quality time off together. We're not sure where we'll go yet, but planning will be part of the fun."

Liz nodded. "I lost a huge client last week, and Greg has been nothing but supportive. I told him I wanted to start refurbishing furniture again, and he's been helping me set up my workshop and watching the boys when I'm working on a new piece. It's the little things that really mean something a lot of the time, you know?"

Everyone smiled and clinked glasses of wine with a cheer.

Donna cleared her throat. "I guess I'll go last. Dale and I had some rocky sections of our relationship, I'll admit. However, when I tell you that I'm falling more in love with this man every day, I'm not joking. He's kind, he's thoughtful, he's hard-working, and most of all, he's loving. He inspires me to be a better person, and for that reason, I can't wait to marry him."

The ladies all clapped and clinked glasses again.

Meanwhile, Margaret walked over to the DVD player. "OK, time for another sappy romance story to finish off the night, or would you prefer a horror movie?"

"No!" Everyone belted out before hysterically laughing.

CHAPTER ELEVEN

The next morning, after all the ladies left, Dave pulled his truck into the driveway.

Margaret peered out of the window, watching him step out of the truck while feeling her heart go abuzz. He looked more handsome than ever, wearing a backwards hat, a white T-shirt, and dirty work jeans and boots. He walked towards the lift gate and reached inside the back, searching for something. Moments later, Margaret burst through the front door and ran towards him, giving him a hug and a kiss as Dave immediately reciprocated and twirled her around.

"What's all this for? How did I get so lucky to receive that welcome home gesture?" Dave asked while smiling.

Margaret stepped away and blew a few stray strands of hair out of her face. "You've been missed so much. You don't even know."

Dave blushed and chuckled. "Trust me. I think I missed you more. Where are the girls?" he asked, looking around the yard.

"They stayed the night with my parents since we had Donna's bachelorette party here last night. They're taking them to Story-book Land and then dinner later. The girls are excited, but I know they're going to be so happy to see you too," Margaret said as she put her arm around Dave's waist and squeezed him towards her.

Dave put his arm around Margaret's shoulders as they walked towards the tractor Margaret had abandoned out of frustration. "I'm rested up and ready to get to work. Where should I start?"

Margaret laughed. "I got the tractor out of the barn, but that's as far it got. I wanted to mow the grass for you, but I couldn't figure it out."

Dave laughed as he hopped in it and immediately got it moving. "Don't worry. I'll take care of it."

Margaret cupped her hands over her mouth. "Dave! One more thing! I know it's not great timing with the wedding, but I invited Frank over for breakfast tomorrow morning with us bright and early."

Dave gave a thumbs-up. "Perfect. More reason for me to hurry up and get all this done."

Margaret waved as Dave drove the tractor towards the front of the house, then she made her way to the big red barn. They really only used the barn to house the tractor, but Margaret wanted to clean up the inside for the wedding.

As Margaret approached the barn, she got a clear vision of what it could look like, and immediately set to work rearranging some items inside and sweeping the floors. There was a lot more to be done that day, but it was starting to come together.

* * *

Over at Animal Outreach, Judy followed behind Bob as they walked through the building, saying hi to volunteers and workers in the process.

Bob approached one of the rooms and peeked inside. "This is where Bruce is. It looks like he's waiting for me," he said with a smile as he let Judy enter first. "Go on and sit in that chair there," Bob said, pointing.

Judy sat down and looked around the room at all the sleeping cats, noticing even more in hidden little corners. Then, she felt it—a light tap on her leg.

"You must be Bruce," Judy said, her face lighting up as she looked down to see the orange tabby staring up at her.

Bruce meowed back at her, then tapped her leg again with his paw.

Bob laughed. "He wants to come up. Pat your lap so he knows it's OK."

Judy patted her lap, and Bruce jumped up to rub his head on her chin as he started kneading her lap and purring. "Wow, he's a lover."

"Well, what do you say? Can we bring him home? They recommend a slow introduction with Hugo, but I think it's meant to be," Bob said as he reached down to scratch Bruce on the head.

"Don't we have to fill out an adoption application?" Judy asked.

"Well, yeah, but I'm sure we'll get approved with our wonderful veterinarian records," Bob said with a wide grin.

Judy laughed. "I see you have your mind made up. I'm all for it. Let's adopt Bruce."

Bob nodded. "I'm thinking he's really going to enjoy looking out the windows at the birds in the backyard."

Judy sighed as she pet Bruce, now curled up in her lap and ready for a long snooze. "I never thought I'd see the day that you would want a cat, but here we are. He's going to be perfect for your long naps in the recliner, I can tell."

* * *

Liz stood out in front of the garage workshop, watching Greg help a couple load up the furniture she'd refurbished into the back of their truck.

"That about does it. Thanks guys," Greg said as he patted the back of the truck. The couple thanked Greg and Liz, then got back into the vehicle.

Greg put his arm around Liz as they watched the truck drive out of sight. "So, how much did you get for that set?"

Liz bit her lip. "Thirty-five hundred."

"You're kidding!" Greg said, staring at Liz, shocked.

Liz laughed and shook her head. "I'm not. Those pieces are highly coveted, and a lot of times they're not in good condition. People will pay for high-quality refurbished vintage furniture."

"I'm absolutely amazed," Greg said as he walked into the garage, noticing she had a mid-century modern kitchen table and chairs sitting there. "Is this finished?"

Liz nodded. "It is. I finished the chairs and table this morning, put it up for sale, and it sold immediately."

"For how much?" Greg asked.

"Thirty-five hundred again," Liz said proudly. "It's the going rate for pieces like this."

"Holy cow. You're killing it!" Greg said, feeling in awe of his wife.

Liz took a seat on a stool and wiped the sweat off her forehead with the back of her arm, then sighed happily. "Greg, I've decided I want to do this full-time. It's giving me a sense of satisfaction that I haven't had with a job in a long time, and I could easily surpass the income I was making as an interior designer."

"You're kidding." Greg was completely taken aback. "So, you're done doing interior design?"

Liz nodded. "I think so. I can always pick it back up in the future should I decide to go back to it, but I'm ready to go all in with this. I just know in my heart that I need to do this right now. I hope that's OK with you …"

Greg walked over to Liz and hugged her tight. "Of course, it's fine. In fact, I urge you to do this if it's what you want."

"There is one thing, though," Liz said sheepishly while looking up at Greg.

"What's that?" Greg asked.

"I might need your help getting furniture from thrift stores to our house and also into buyers' vehicles. That part I can't really do on my own," Liz said.

Greg laughed. "We can work something out, but if you start finding a lot of furniture, it might be time to hire an assistant. I'm not sure how long my back will last for that."

"Of course. That's the plan," Liz said as she watched another truck pull into their driveway. "But first, we have to get this kitchen table and chairs into that truck."

* * *

The waves crashed along the shoreline, but out in the ocean, where Lisa and the rest of the surfers were, it was serene and quiet. The sun was shining brightly, and Lisa smiled as she watched some kids dip buckets into the shallow end of the water, then run back to the sandy section of the beach where their parents were, spilling most of the water on the way. Just then, a tall man came into view. He held a surfboard while talking with the lifeguard. She squinted to get a better look but realized it was Nick when he turned towards her. She immediately felt a tinge of excitement run through her body as she watched him walk in the ocean, then start paddling out her way.

"I thought I'd catch you out here," he said as he paddled up next to her, then sat on his board, letting his legs dangle off either side.

"How'd you know?" Lisa, smiled.

Nick shrugged. "It's too nice of day to not surf … though not a wave to be seen out here, huh?"

Lisa shook her head. "There's nothing. Maybe a wave big enough once every ten minutes. Mostly, I've just been meditating out here and thinking about life."

Nick laughed. "One of my favorite things to do on a board besides surf."

Lisa laughed with him, and then they both grew quiet. "You know, I've been thinking—"

Nick cut in quickly. "I've been thinking too. Are we …?"

"In a relationship?" Lisa asked.

Nick blushed. "How'd you know I was going to ask that?"

Lisa bit her lip. "I had a hunch."

"Well, I've been afraid to ask. I wasn't sure how you'd feel about that," Nick said as he ran his hand through the water.

Lisa shielded her eyes from the sun with her hand. "It's funny because I've been wondering the same thing about us."

Nick moved his board closer to Lisa. "Do you want to be in a relationship with me?"

Lisa laughed over the absurdity of the situation. "Why does this feel like first grade? This is so awkward," she said turning to Nick to look him in the eye. "Nick, are you asking me to be your girlfriend?"

Nick reached over to hold Lisa's hand. "Yes, and I'd give you a lollipop to show my true affection, like in first grade, but I don't have any," he said while smiling.

Lisa sighed happily. "Yes, I'd like to be in an exclusive relationship with you."

Nick grinned from ear to ear. "Good, because I don't know what I would have done if you said no. I'm too invested in this."

Just then, they heard a commotion behind them and noticed the other surfers giving a heads-up about a nice-sized wave coming at them. Lisa and Nick both paddled furiously to catch it, and they both managed to stand up and ride the wave out to the shoreline.

Nick, dripping wet with water, picked up his board and put his hand up to Lisa for a high five. "You ready to get back out there and ride a couple more?"

Lisa ran her fingers through her long hair and adjusted her bathing suit. "You know it."

* * *

Over at the Book Nook, Sarah hosted their first event outside in the backyard. It was called Coffee and Herbs with the class focusing on potting and caring for culinary herbs and learning how to use them in cooking. There were twenty-five participants in attendance, and the teacher, Roseann, seemed delighted to be there.

"This space is wonderful, Sarah," Roseann said as she set up a bag of potting soil next to each chair. "This is the type of class you actually want to do outside. I'd be worried about the mess we'd make inside."

Sarah smiled and nodded. "I'm glad this all worked out because we just discovered we had this amazing space the other day. Got it fixed up in a jiffy so we could host events and discussions out here. I'm really happy with it," she said sipping her coffee and admiring the pink rosebushes growing over the side of the fence.

Roseann nodded and placed the potted herbs on the table as Sarah sighed happily.. Startled when she felt someone's arms embrace her from behind, she looked back to see Chris.

"Hey, you," Chris said, "thought I'd stop by to see what you did out here."

Sarah hugged him. "How do you like it?"

Chris did a chef's kiss. "I love it. It's nice to get some fresh air while you're learning, no?"

Sarah nodded. "Definitely, and it will be nice to free up

space in the shop so customers can easily get to the bookshelves without the table and chairs blocking them."

"So, what's on the roster? Any events I would like to attend?" Chris asked half-jokingly.

Sarah shrugged. "We've got knitting, crocheting, sourdough bread baking, woodworking, and the list goes on."

Chris laughed. "Sounds like quite a lineup."

Sarah nudged him. "How's Eric? Is he still running a booze cruise over there?" she jokingly asked.

Chris shook his head and smiled. "Nah, Eric is doing fine. We had to work out a few learning kinks, but today I let him run a birding cruise all on his own. I was on the boat with him, but I didn't do any of the talking or navigating. He managed to find all the perfect spots to see birds and was very talkative and informative with the guests. He knows a lot, and I think he's a great addition to Blue Heron Birding Boats."

"That's really great to hear," Sarah said as she watched the class participants start to file outside, all sipping drinks they had bought inside.

"You've got a good thing going here," Chris said as he watched the students take their seats at the table. "By the way, Eric is taking over the birding cruises tomorrow by himself while we're at the wedding. I think he's all set to handle it."

Sarah smiled and looked at Chris. "Are you ready for the wedding? Did you get your suit dry-cleaned?"

Chris nodded. "I did. Everything is ready. So, no bridal party, eh?"

Sarah shook her head. "Nope. Donna didn't want one. Personally, I don't blame her. It takes the pressure off others. I might do the same when we get married, but honestly, lately I've been thinking I want to elope."

Chris's mouth dropped open. "Elope?"

Sarah laughed. "OK, maybe not elope, but probably a destination wedding and whoever can come, can come."

Chris chuckled. "When were you going to tell me about this idea?"

Sarah shrugged. "I don't know. I only started thinking about it a week ago. I know you probably want something more traditional."

Chris shook his head. "I did at first, but the more I think about it, the more I just want us to pick the least stressful option that fulfills us the most. I've been to a few really great destination weddings. That has my vote."

Sarah felt so happy, she could burst. "Let's have our wedding next year. A destination wedding."

"So, we're making this big decision right now and right here, next to this herbal class?" Chris said while laughing.

"Why not?" Sarah asked as she took a sip of her iced coffee and smiled.

CHAPTER TWELVE

Margaret peered out the window at Dave, who was walking inside from the yard.

"It's looking great out there," Margaret said as she pulled the egg frittata and baked French toast out of the oven.

Dave nodded as he looked back out the window. "The gang all worked pretty hard last night hanging decorations after the rehearsal dinner with Donna and Dale. It's all come together nicely."

Margaret flipped over the bacon in the sizzling pan. "Did I just see a truck drop off tables and chairs?"

"Yep. They're all set up and ready to go. It's early yet, but later the florist, bakery, caterers, and everyone else will be arriving. For now, I'm starving," Dave said, eyeing the scrumptious breakfast she made.

"Frank should be over any moment. His son is joining us," Margaret said just as a knock came at the back door.

Dave got up to answer it. "Nice to meet you, Frank, I'm Dave. Sorry we haven't met yet."

Frank smiled and shook Dave's hand then pointed to his son. "This is Carl, my son."

"Nice to meet you, Carl. You in town for the holiday?"

Margaret asked as she started placing the dishes in the middle of the set table in the kitchen.

Carl shrugged. "I'm not quite sure how long I'm staying."

Frank cut in. "He's going through a divorce."

"Thanks, Dad," Carl said with a chuckle.

"Margaret and I both have been divorced before. It's not fun, but you'll get through," Dave said as he sat in a chair at the table.

"Please, sit," Margaret said as she took a seat next to Dave. "I've got orange juice and water to drink. And help yourself to all the food. We have plenty. Dig in!"

"This is simply incredible," Frank said as he scooped French toast onto his plate.

"So, it looks like you're having an event here. I saw the tables and chairs being delivered earlier," Carl said as he poured orange juice into his glass.

Dave took a bite of the egg frittata. "Our good friends are getting married this evening, and they asked if they could have the wedding on our property."

Margaret nodded. "We apologize if the music gets loud tonight."

Frank waved his hand in the air. "Don't worry about that. I can't hear well anyway." He chuckled.

Everyone at the table laughed along with Frank.

An hour later, they were finished eating and talking, and Frank stood up and cleared his throat. "Do you have some time for me to show you some interesting things on your property?"

Dave's eyes lit up. "Definitely. We still have a few hours before any other vendors arrive. What did you have in mind?"

"Got that golf cart handy? I'd like to head towards the greenhouse and lighthouse," Frank said as he approached the back door.

Five minutes later, they got out of the golf cart and stood around the lighthouse, looking it up and down.

"Is it alright if I go inside?" Frank asked as he opened the door and looked in.

"Sure, go ahead," Margaret said as they all followed him inside.

Once inside, Frank racked his brain, searching different corners of the room. "I know it was in here. I remember it."

Carl furrowed his brow. "What was in here, Pop?"

Frank didn't answer, instead did a little hop when he spotted four large star tiles amid the wooden floor. "This is it," he said, pointing.

"Yes, we've always loved those tiles," Dave said as he stood next to Frank. "Never really understood why they were there since it's a wood floor but ..."

Frank kneeled down. "I'll show you why they're there ... Carl, can you come help me?"

Carl crouched next to Frank and they gently lifted the four large tiles up to reveal stairs going down into the ground.

Margret and Dave gasped in shock. "Is that a wine cellar?"

Frank nodded happily. "It is. Well, it's more of a root cellar, but they stored wine down here too. I knew my memory wasn't failing me after all these years."

"Do you think it's safe to go down?" Dave asked as he peered into the cool darkness.

"Hard to say, but it might be worth a try if what I think is in there still is," Frank said.

They all carefully walked down the steps, using the flash-lights on their phones, and immediately noticed very old jars of canned vegetables.

"My gosh, these jars could very well be fifty years old or more at this point," Frank said, picking one up.

"Look, are those wine bottles?" Margaret asked, pointing ahead.

Dave walked over and picked one up. "They've never been opened."

Carl scoured the room, locating some old paintings

leaning against a wall, but Frank wasn't satisfied. There was one thing he was hoping to find that they hadn't seen yet. Then, there it was—a large wooden box behind the paintings.

"Grab that box and bring it upstairs," Frank said as he started to head towards the stairs and out of the root cellar.

Carl picked it up, noticing it was quite light, and followed Margaret and Dave upstairs.

Frank took a seat in the lone wooden chair and opened the box that Carl set in front of him. As soon as he lifted the lid, it was like he saw gold. His eyes lit up with excitement.

"What's in there, Frank?" Margaret asked, growing more curious by the minute.

Frank swallowed. "Old photos from when I worked on the farm on your property," he said, then handed a few to Margaret and Dave. "You'll want to see these ... but that's not what I'm really excited about." Frank pulled out stacks and stacks of small little envelopes with writing on the front. "These here, these are rare heirloom seeds for all types of vegetables we used to grow. I'm pretty sure a lot of them are deemed extinct, as I've looked some of them up and can't find them. You don't see the seeds sold anymore, but that can all change now ..."

"Wow," Dave said as he picked up an envelope and looked inside. "You think they're still good? We can plant these?"

Frank shrugged. "Seeds can last years, but they do lose their germination rates as the years go on. I've heard of fifty-year-old seeds growing, though. You may be able to get a few out of the envelope to germinate. In fact, bringing back these heirlooms may very well lie in your hands. These could be the only seeds of these varieties left in the world."

Margaret chuckled. "I suddenly feel a ton of pressure to do this right."

Dave smiled. "I'm really excited to see what we can do with these. We'll have to make sure we do it right. The plants will have to be far enough apart so there isn't any cross-pollination."

Frank stood up from the chair. "I'm amazed it was still here after all of this time. It's like finding a time capsule."

"Why don't we leave the pictures with you for now," Margaret said.

"That would be great, but the seeds, that's all you guys. I'll take some of the seeds from your first harvest," Frank said as he walked out of the lighthouse.

Dave stood beside Frank, marveling at the seeds he was holding. "So, what all is there to know about this land? Anymore hidden treasures?"

Frank smiled and paused for a moment in thought. "This land has a rich history. Like I told Margaret, I was employed here when it was a working farm. I plowed the fields and harvested the orchards and gardens. I would say I did that for about five years before I got a better job, but as far as treasures, they're all around you out here … in every nook and cranny. I'm told this area is a hot spot for mushroom foraging. I've seen people trespassing to look for mushrooms and ramps. They were over in that forested area of your property a few years ago. Haven't seen them since."

"Really?" Margaret said, overhearing the conversation. "We haven't spent much time in the woods yet."

Frank nodded. "Well, you should. Just educate yourselves about foraging and mushrooms. There are many that are not safe to eat. I've also been told there's some pawpaws back there. Anyway, I could go on and on about how special this land is from the old tall oaks to the perfect growing soil and everything in between. I'm looking forward to seeing what you do with those seeds. I know they're in good hands with you two. Next time we get together, we'll go over more of the wonderful history of your property, but for now, I'm ready for a little nap," Frank said, yawning. He started walking towards the golf cart with the rest of them trailing behind.

Margaret glanced at Dave, wondering if he felt as giddy as she did about everything Frank had said. Dave glanced back with a smile, and she immediately knew he was just as thrilled. They had picked the perfect home, and now it wasn't even debatable.

* * *

By 6 p.m., one hundred wedding guests had arrived, and by 6:30 p.m., the ceremony was underway. Dale and Donna were married in front of Margaret's beautiful flower garden. Donna held a bouquet of sunflowers and wore her gorgeous vintage wedding gown while Dale donned a traditional black tuxedo. They both looked amazing and happy. After their vows, they were pronounced man and wife and bowed to their friends and family, who were clapping and cheering. They left to take wedding photos around the yard while everyone else walked over to the cocktail hour.

Donna and Dale stood in front of the tall rows of purple and blue larkspur, waiting for the photographer as she cleaned the camera lens. "Give me one minute, you two," the photographer said as she searched through her bag.

"You look incredible," Dale said as he picked up Donna's hand and kissed it.

Donna smiled. "So do you. Can you believe we're married? You're now my husband," she said, giggling.

"Yes, my wife, that's correct," Dale said with a slight chuckle.

"OK, how about we start with a serious pose," the photographer cut in as she held her camera to her face.

By the time it was dark, the reception had officially started, and the property transformed. All along the yard, lit luminaries lined different pathways, and above in the sky were battery-operated taper candles, hanging from trees. In other trees were hanging paper moons and stars lit by uplights on the ground.

Then, on the tables, the decorated mason jars Donna had put together held flower bouquets with wands sticking out. The magic theme was magical, especially at night.

A band was playing inside the barn with half the guests dancing and the other half still finishing their meals out at the tables under the oak tree. It was the perfect summer wedding. The lightning bugs floated around the yard, and the mosquitos left most of the guests alone, probably thanks to the citronella candles that had been placed in different areas of the property.

At 9 p.m., the band took a break, and the magic show began to the surprise of most of the guests. Jack Jeffries took the microphone and corralled everyone into the barn. The white string lights dimmed, and the purple and blue uplights turned on. Then, Jack and Tracy put on one of the best shows anyone in the audience had seen. It didn't have all of the special effects like fire and smoke that were normally seen at professional venues, but there was a ton of audience participation, which made it feel more intimate and personal. Almost everyone got involved with the magic tricks, including the newlyweds.

The magic show went on for an hour, and right before Jack concluded, he asked everyone to follow him out of the barn and into the open field next to it. He looked at his watch, held his hands in the air, and as soon as he dropped them, the first Fourth of July fireworks went off in the distance. Then, they kept going off, lighting up the sky with all sorts of colors. Everyone clapped and cheered, excited for such a great view.

Afterwards, the band played again and most of the guests squeezed into the barn, kicking off their shoes and dancing like they hadn't danced before.

Donna wrapped her arms around Dale as they danced with their friends and family, then leaned into his ear. "I'm a little hot. Do you want to take a walk with me?"

Dale nodded, took her hand, and they walked out of the crowded, noisy barn into the yard, strolling amongst the luminaries and out towards the greenhouse past the pond. It wasn't a short walk, but Donna needed the cool air for a moment.

"I love this part of their yard," Donna said to Dale as they walked towards the creek, hearing it gurgle behind the bushes and trees.

Dale looked first towards the lighthouse, and then the greenhouse, noticing something in the windows. "Do you see that? What is it?"

They headed over to the greenhouse to find that someone had put battery-operated candles of different heights all over the potting tables inside. In the middle of the candles was a handwritten note with rose petals around it. They read the note together: *Enjoy the moment. Enjoy the memories. Enjoy the magic.*

"This is so sweet. Do you think Margaret and Dave did this?" Donna asked.

Dale peered out the door to see Margaret and Dave sneaking into the lighthouse across from them. "Maybe, but you can ask them right now if you want," he said, pointing.

Donna led Dale to the lighthouse and peeked her head through the doorway. "Hey, guys?"

"Ow," Margaret said, after bumping her head on the low ceiling. "We're down here."

Donna and Dale followed the voices down the steps and into the root cellar. "Whoa, you didn't tell me about this cool little space," Donna said, eyeing up the many jars of canned beets, carrots, and string beans.

"Our neighbor just told us about it this morning, and we can't stop thinking about it. We decided to take a break from dancing to see what else we could find," Margaret said as she moved some jars to look behind them.

"Mind if we help look? I'm totally into this stuff," Dale said, while shining his cell phone's flashlight through the shelves.

"Not at all," Dave said as he picked up a painting off the floor and studied it.

Donna gasped. "That's incredible. Look out how the ship is navigating those angry waves in that painting. It's impeccable."

Dale nodded in agreement. "Hey, by the way, did you guys put all of those candles in the greenhouse?"

Margaret smiled. "We did. We figured somebody would make their way out here tonight and wanted to doll up our favorite part of the yard. We're glad it was you two. Congratulations on your perfect wedding day."

Dale and Donna smiled, then looked at each other and kissed. They hadn't expected to be in a dark root cellar on their wedding night looking at paintings and expired canned food and wine, but it was the perfect adventure to kick off their life together.

EPILOGUE

It was mid-July and hot and humid in Cape May. Margaret picked tomatoes out of the garden and gently piled the different colored varieties into her basket. After finishing, she walked towards the back door, but stopped to rip a large bunch of fragrant basil off.

Once in the kitchen, she found her two favorite tomatoes, a lemon boy and a black krim. She washed them off, then sliced the juicy tomatoes on the cutting board before sprinkling flaky salt on them. Then she sliced her freshly baked crusty sourdough bread. It smelled amazing in the kitchen. She pulled out her homemade mayonnaise from the fridge, then swiped the bread slices with it before piling on the tomatoes and basil. She poured two glasses of homemade lemonade and set them on a tray with the two plated sandwiches, and headed out the front door.

"What's this?" Dave asked happily as he set down a piece of lumber.

"I made us tomato sandwiches fresh from the garden. Everything on it is homemade. I figured you could take a little break and we could have lunch together," Margaret said as she found a piece of grass to sit on.

"This looks delicious," Dave said as he took a bite, then washed it down with lemonade. "Best tomato sandwich I've ever had. By the way … what do you think of all of this," he said pointing behind him.

Margaret laughed. "So, we're really doing this? We're building our own farm stand?"

Dave smiled. "Yes, that's what we agreed upon."

"I know. I know. I just can't believe it's actually happening," Margaret said as she took a sip of her lemonade.

Dave nodded as he looked at the lumber scattered around them and the circular saw off to the side. "I'm thinking it could be the same size as our old one over at Liz and Greg's … or maybe bigger?"

"Bigger?" Margaret asked as her eyes widened.

Dave laughed. "OK, maybe not bigger, but I'm glad we're going ahead with this. I miss stocking that little stand with produce, and meeting the town folk and vacationers who would stop by. We have some good memories there."

Margaret sighed. "I miss it too. My gosh, we're going to have so much food to stock it with. When do you think you'll be finished?"

Dave sighed. "If my brother comes over to help like he said he would, I think we could be done by early August. It'll be the size of a run-in shed, except we're going to build raised benches to put in it. That's where the baskets of tomatoes and other produce can go."

Margaret looked back at the house, then back at Dave. "It seems like a nice place to put it. It's in the front of our property but off to the side, about a half-acre away from the house."

"That's what I was thinking," Dave said as he finished his sandwich. "By the way, what is going on with the farm stand at Liz and Greg's house? Are they still keeping it stocked?"

Margaret shook her head. "They did last year, but this year I think all the extra produce has been going to Greg's restaurant and probably Dale's restaurant too." Margaret paused in thought, then laughed. "I have way too many ventures. The tea garden, the Seahorse Inn, my job at Pinetree … Luckily, the farm stand will operate on the honor system for payments so we don't have to be there."

"But it will still be fun to be at the farm stand sometimes. How else will we meet anyone that passes through?" Dave asked as he kneeled down to pick up a piece of lumber and heaved it over his shoulder.

"You're right. Getting involved with the community is a great joy in life. We'll find a way to spend more time at the farm stand, I'm sure," Margaret said as she stood up, brushed the grass off of her, then closed her eyes just as a summer breeze blew through and cooled her off for a moment.

* * *

Pick up **Book 15** in the Cape May Series**, Cape May Glitter,** to follow Margaret, Liz, the rest of the familiar bunch, and some new characters.

Visit my website at www.claudiavance.com

ABOUT THE AUTHOR

Claudia Vance is a writer of women's fiction and clean romance. She writes feel good reads that take you to places you'd like to visit with characters you'd want to get to know.

She lives with her boyfriend and two cats in a charming small town in New Jersey, not too far from the beautiful beach town of Cape May. She worked behind the scenes on television shows and film sets for many years, and she's an avid gardener and nature lover.

This is a work of fiction. Names, places, events, organizations, characters, and businesses are used in a fictitious manner or the product of the author's imagination.